A BARD AND ROGUE'S TALE

SHERIDAN N. GILLAM

CONTENTS

For all the queers who love an adventure.

With the strength of my friends...

...I shall descend into the dragon's den.

CHAPTER 1

THE UGLY NECKLACE

The night cloaked Razil in darkness as her feet whispered along the cobbled road, careful to move in the shadows like an apparition. She did not understand her true objective, only that the stifling heat of the blacksmith's workshop left some desire for her old life. As much as she hated this part of her being, it lit a fire in her stomach that little else could.

Razil approached her destination with apprehension, knowing she would need to pass The Red Dragon Inn before arriving. This path would be safer than going around the castle or coliseum; however, the tavern would be bustling with people this time of night, and she needed to remain undetected for the heist to succeed.

A couple, drunk in love, swayed as they approached Razil's position along the path. She gently hugged the tavern wall, pulled her cloak tighter over her head, and held her breath behind the black mask that only left her eyes visible.

The two men giggled as they wobbled side to side, hand-in-hand. Razil pressed tighter against the tavern wall. Luckily, the night was cloudy, and the moonlight would not give away her position. The music of a lute caressed her ear from the dusty window to her right. Razil recognized the tune and knew her gnomish friend was behind the beautiful strumming.

The men began dancing, holding each other close. It was a clumsy dance as the taller man rested his chin on the shorter man's bald head, causing his beard to fold over the other man's head like a poorly made wig. Razil realized they would be here for a while, and she did not have much time before the gladiator match at the coliseum would be over. Once it ended, the nobles and wealth of Gar Thanik would return to their dwellings. If she was going to rob Councilor Genna Landcaster, her window of opportunity was rapidly closing.

Slowly, Razil began shuffling her feet, timing each step with the beat of the music. The men danced and stomped as she slipped from the tavern wall unnoticed. Razil sprinted along the path with a soft pitter-patter, keeping to the grass lining the cobbled road. Her pulse raced as sweat began to coat the nape of her neck, the hair starting to plaster onto her skin.

As she approached the councilor's headquarters, she consciously slowed her breathing and heart rate. Razil scanned the building, looking for her ideal entry point. It had a stone first story with large windows where meetings and official business took place. The entrance was marked by a bulky wooden door with two guards standing tall in their knight's armor.

Razil sank to the ground with her belly snug against the dewy grass. Though she was confident she would win a squabble with these two guards, she wanted to complete the robbery without spilling blood. Had she still been under Wolf's control, he would have expected a quick slit of the throat, with the bodies later discarded in Blue Lake.

She shuddered, remembering the handful of bodies slain by her hand. Razil had never known who she killed, that time of her life locked away in a bubble of survival and self-pity, but her previous boss had. She just knew she was hungry and they were not, she had holes in her clothes and they did not, she was trapped under a tyrant trying to provide for her mother and herself, and they were not. But Wolf, he knew and he picked his targets. She just executed his bidding.

The memory of their lifeless eyes still haunted her. If it could be avoided, she would never use such measures again. She shook off the memories of her past and put her mind back to the task at hand.

She would be stealthy enough to pull this off undetected or bail tonight. Her focus and daring would be her success, and she fought to regain it.

Razil began by squinting to inspect the building further. She peered at the second story, framed in wooden beams. According to Wolf's blueprints she'd seen when she was a member of his thieves' guild, The Wolf's Teeth, this was where Genna's living quarters were supposed to be. Razil was certain that Genna's quarters were on the east end of the building, but something in her gut was pulling her to the west window with a small flower box resting on the outside. Wolf's blueprints had been wrong in the past, and the feeling pulling her towards the west end was strong.

Razil rarely ignored her gut and began unhooking the grappling hook and rope from her belt. She crawled along the grass, careful to match her movements to the typical rustling of creatures of the night. The guards stood like stone, unaware of her movements. She reached the west window without so much as a turn of the head from either guard. An unexpected pride filled Razil at the feat.

The grappling hook would be another issue. The sound of the metal clanging against the window would need to be timed perfectly.

Luckily, the gladiator's match from the coliseum was loud enough that its sound permeated to the castle and the councilor's headquarters, which were neatly tucked behind its massive oval structure. She would time her throw with the sound of applause and cheers.

Each moment passed like mud trapped in an hourglass. Still, Razil remained patient, grappling hook in hand. Finally, the thunderous applause reached her position, and she released the grappling hook. It hit the window's ledge, and she pulled tight to ensure it was secure. Razil made her ascent, quickly shimmying up the rope before anyone noticed. When she reached the window, she was happy to find it unlocked and pushed herself through.

The room was dark. Only the sound of her boots lightly creaking against the wooden floor was audible as Razil stepped into the room. Genna was at the gladiator's match, and based on the quiet darkness, her daughter must have been there as well.

Razil studied the room as her eyes adjusted to the darkness. She noticed a large, cushiony bed positioned centrally against the far back wall with a bedside table and several bookshelves filled to the brim. A large desk resided across the room from the bed, and its organized manner contrasted with the spilling bookshelves. Razil stalked towards the bedside table, hoping to find something of value, only to find a painting that made her stomach plummet. Razil grabbed it hastily and brought it close to her face so she could confirm who it was, even though she was pretty sure.

The painting depicted a blonde woman with long, wavy hair in a colorful dress hanging on what looked like the councilor's daughter's arm. The longer Razil stared, the more she realized she was, in fact, looking at a picture of Alyssandra Landcaster and her ex-lover, Yurenda Cawll. Razil was in the wrong bedroom; she should've ignored her gut instinct and gone to the east end. Razil rallied her spirits and put down the painting. She still had time to get to Councilor Landcaster's bedroom and find spoils of jewels.

A flicker of light caught Razil's eye as her shadow became visible on the wall—right next to the silhouette of another figure.

She spun to find a beautiful woman holding a torch in one hand and a dagger in the other. Razil gasped, her stomach in knots, grabbing for her saber in vain. The woman had her pinned against the wall with her blade before Razil could unsheathe her weapon. Razil blinked back her dreaded surprise and realized the woman restraining her was Alyssandra Landcaster.

Alyssandra's maroon dress hugged her hourglass frame like a glove, and her embroidered sleeves entranced Razil with their swift movement. Razil snapped out of her fixation, controlling her breathing and eying the room for spoils and an escape. When she tried to turn her head, the cool metal of Alyssandra's dagger became an unwelcome reminder of where it resided.

Like a breath on her neck, the blade left a curious space between Razil's ribs where her heart drummed quicker and her lungs slowed. Razil narrowed her eyes, taking in Alyssandra's bronze skin and raven black hair. Razil did not fear the other woman, the deviant in her relishing the unspoken challenge. After all, her opponent was a Landcaster and more versed in dresses and fancy dinners than a battle of the blade.

Razil glared at Alyssandra, whose shallow breath hissed between the small gap in her front teeth. Her dark brown eyes bore into her, but Razil did not waver, staring straight back, daring Alyssandra to pull closer. Daring her to attack, though Razil doubted she actually would. Razil maintained the close proximity she was seemingly trapped in, but her true intention lingered across Alyssandra's ornate bedroom on her desk. Perhaps the initial surprise and her misstep would pay off after all.

The light from Alyssandra's torch illuminated the object, and it was all Razil could think of. It had a golden chain and its jewel was a garish red. The hideous necklace oozed privilege, sparkling and seducing Razil to claim it as her own. The rogue in Razil would both live in Alyssandra's mind, etched as a phantom, and steal her ugly necklace. Of this, Razil was sure.

"Give me a reason why I should not kill you where you stand," Alyssandra demanded, her voice sultry.

This woman was beautiful. Even with a blade to her neck, Razil could not help but take in her curves and delicately fierce oval face. Her thick lips drew Razil in, but she remained focused on the task and knew she would not deviate from stealing from her, beautiful or not.

"Many women find me charming. Perhaps you will find the same and release your blade from my neck. Not that I do not appreciate the beauty of a woman pinning me to a wall." Razil tried to slip from behind Alyssandra's dagger as she said it.

Alyssandra held the dagger closer, almost tight enough to draw blood. "Careful, foolish rogue. My dagger holds a poison that would kill you in minutes if it were to enter your bloodstream. Your supposed charm is that of an ogre's breath. Why are you here?"

Razil squinted. "To rob you, of course."

"Are you one of Wolf's?"

"I am not," Razil said while mulling over her options to escape her predicament. The bravado she was exuding to entertain Alyssandra was exhausting her patience.

"Do not lie to me, thief! Do you think I am a fool? Only Wolf would be brazen enough to steal from a Landcaster." Alyssandra's cheeks reddened, and her eyes were filled with rage.

Realizing her taunting may have gone too far, Razil decided that her only option for escape was to do something repulsive. She bit down on her back molar, which hid a capsule of the most disgusting powder she knew would leave bitterness on her tongue for days. As Alyssandra leaned in closer to yell at her further, Razil dropped her mask and spat the blinding powder into Alyssandra's face.

Razil had thirty seconds before Alyssandra would regain her sight. Alyssandra pawed at her eyes and screamed in horror. Tears streamed down her face as her eyes turned a hideous red. A snot bubble escaped the beautiful woman's nose as every orifice of her body leaked desperate fluid. Alyssandra was no doubt excruciatingly burning and temporarily blinded. Razil knew the sensible thing would be to escape out of the window immediately. But this night had not been born of sensibility.

"What have you done to me?" Alyssandra screeched as she dropped to her knees.

"Do not fear. You will not be blinded for long," Razil chided as she sprinted to the desk. Her curiosity could not let it be. Pocketing the necklace, she ran to the window, pulling her mask over her nose. She slipped out the window, one hand wrapped around the rope and the other holding onto the ledge. As she was about to exit, she felt a harsh pull on her arm.

Alyssandra, with bloodshot eyes, was yanking at her arm as Razil's body hung halfway out the window. Razil shook her hand free of her elbow-length glove, causing Alyssandra to fall backward. Quickly, Razil scurried down the wall and made her escape, running into the night.

CHAPTER 2

A LUTE FOR YOUR TROUBLES

The Red Dragon Inn was busting at the seams with people talking loudly and laughing, spittle jumping from their drunken jowls as they did. Zippy's nostrils filled with the smell of hops and hearty stew. It made his mouth water as he made his way to Wes Trendon at the bar, each step slightly stickier than the last.

Wes had his back to Zippy, pouring a beer from the tap for an overly sweaty gentleman who was bracing himself on the bar's ledge. When he turned and handed the beer to the man, the drunkard stumbled away, allowing Zippy to step up to the bar. The bar's ledge met his forehead, and he stood on tiptoes to peer over the ledge into Wes' dark brown eyes. Being a gnome in a human town was a challenge at times.

Wes smiled in a way that made the wrinkles in worn skin crinkle more deeply around his eyes. He lightly ran a hand over the short black curls on his head before resting it on the hefty leather belt around his waist.

"Zippy, my boy! Quite a crowd you're playing for tonight. My friend, you and that lute have already brought in coin."

Zippy smiled and peered over his shoulder at his lute and jar, which was already filled with coins, resting on the stage against the center back wall of the tavern. If only Wes knew just how magical that lute really was. He was under the impression that Zippy's talent was what made him so much coin.

"You need a beer to wet your whistle for the next song?"

"You know me well, dear friend," Zippy said with an exaggerated bow.

Of all the living arrangements Zippy had experienced over the years, living under Wes' roof was not one to scoff at. Zippy just had to keep the coin coming, which, with the help of his magical lute, was not an issue, and he got the nicest room upstairs and three square meals a day. The nights were tied up with music, but Zippy's days were his own. He was free to wander and meander as he wished. He had friends and an orange cat that visited his windowsill every night that he now considered his pet. Even so, he knew this would not be his forever home. In his three hundred years of existence, nothing ever had been.

The beer Wes set in front of him was light and hoppy, just like he preferred. He sipped it delicately, letting the bubbles tickle his throat. He gave Wes a wink and headed back to the stage where his lute lay in wait. He set down his beer to pick up his lute and began strumming. He seldom knew what song he would play next, letting his fingers decide how they wished to strum. He was surprised by the tune they picked, but did not fight it as he began to sing.

From the meadows, I was born,

And a jolly gnome I was, but the meadows weren't enough.

My family's disappointed eyes,

All I carry from the burrows.

The lonely traveler is I.

To Leedbriar I went,

> *Magic entrancing every step.*
> *I found the love of friendship,*
> *The lonely traveler is I.*
> *Kindrelve of the Dwarfs,*
> *He took me in like a son,*
> *Singing in the mines.*
> *The lonely traveler is I.*
> *The horses in the field,*
> *The skeptical human eye,*
> *I loved the smell of the flowers.*
> *The lonely traveler is I.*
> *Where am I now?*
> *Where am I to go?*
> *I know not who I am.*
> *The lonely traveler is I.*

Zippy's eyes teared at the last line, but he quickly sniffed it back at the sound of coins jingling heavily in the jar before him. The stronger he felt, the more effective the magic from his lute. It was apparent this particular song stirred deep emotion, given the number of hands throwing coins into his jar.

All except for one. She must have snuck in when he was playing. She was Zippy's greatest friend in Gar Thanik and somehow immune to his tune. He suspected it was the amulet she always wore around her neck. She seldom displayed it, as it rested under her shirt, but he could sense the magical energy emanating from her chest.

Razil Morganth smiled at him and clapped her hands in gentle applause. One hand was gloved while the other was bare, revealing a calloused, tanned hand. She was one of the only people who knew the magic he possessed, outside of their friend Dracklin. If the rest of the city knew they were being magically manipulated out of their coin, his exit from the city would be swift and final. And though he knew he would eventually leave, he wasn't ready yet.

Zippy set down his lute, earning an annoyed look from Wes. He usually expected more than one song before Zippy went on break again. Zippy raised his eyebrows at him and shook the clanging coins in the jar in front of him. Wes threw up his hands in surrender, and Zippy bounded in Razil's direction with a chuckle.

His chuckle was soon stifled when he looked closer at his friend. Her ear-length blonde hair was dripping with sweat, and her blue eyes, normally large and soft like the ripple of a stream, were hardened like ice. She was in all black, and her breath smelled of blinding powder. Worst of all, there was a telltale bulge in her pocket that to most may look like a tobacco tin, but was most likely something stolen.

"Not this again, Razil," Zippy said, concern dripping from his tongue.

"Zippy Redbeard, what exactly am I not doing again?" Razil asked nonchalantly as she signaled at Wes' brother, Heathsworth, to bring her a beer.

"Tell me you're not working with Wolf again, Razil," Zippy said, eying her pocket pointedly.

Razil crossed her arms and did not make eye contact with him. Several quiet seconds passed. Razil glanced around the room before taking off her one glove and recrossing her arms.

"One day, this reluctance to give up your old ways fully is going to get the best of you, Razil, and I will not be there to help you," Zippy said. He saw the lost look dancing in Razil's eyes and knew he did not mean the statement.

She crammed her glove in the same pocket as the already bulging one, giving it a comical look. She looked like a child trying to steal sweets from the counter. Zippy rocked on his feet, patiently awaiting her reply before bombarding her with more judgment.

"Zippy, I do not expect you to fight my battles. I do not expect you to fight any battles really, you're not very tall or strong. But rest assured, I am not dabbling in The Wolf's Teeth again, if that's what you think. All harmless fun, I promise you," Razil said with a pained wince followed by a haphazard wink. She began chugging the beer that Heathsworth handed to her. The barman looked between them and scooted away awkwardly, clearly sensing the tension.

Zippy knew he had to play this right. Razil was an introvert by nature and one who did not trust easily, only coming out of her shell when she felt safe or when she needed to woo a beautiful woman. "I do not know how you drink that dark beer so hastily, friend. It's like shoving a rich cake down in one bite."

Razil's ice began to melt from her eyes. "Dear friend, the darker the beer, the better. It's smoother and has a flavor that light fluff cannot match." She paused and looked at him more sincerely. "I am not working with Wolf again, I promise, but I also do not wish to speak further on what you think you know of my whereabouts tonight."

He felt she was telling the truth. If she was stealing, at least it was of her own accord and not for that ruthless vulture again. "Sing a song with me, my strange, dark beer-drinking friend."

Razil snickered. "We both know I do not sing, Zippy."

"Come on, the crowd is drunk. We'll pick a favorite that will get them singing. No one will even hear how tone-deaf you are." He waggled his eyebrows at her.

Razil rolled her eyes at his constant eyebrow movements and gestured towards the stage. "Lead the way, little friend." She then looked at Wes while hoisting her beer in the air and said, "This one better be on the house for this."

Wes laughed and gave a thumbs-up.

Zippy picked up his lute and began playing a familiar tune. Razil stood tensely next to him but relaxed as the crowd hummed along to the familiar somber melody. The chorus would be easy, the song of the red dragon being a crowd favorite. Zippy took a deep breath through his nose and began singing.

> *The dragon of old*
> *Dancing in the sky,*
> *Meeting the blade of our ancestors,*
> *To die in the sky.*
> *I fear no more,*
> *For my fair country is free,*
> *From the knights who came before us,*
> *Died that we might be.*

The crowd swayed and sang the last verse with proud vindication. Zippy looked at Razil out of the corner of his eye, relieved to see her usual energy had returned. She hopped off the stage with a soft thud.

"I must retire for the night. The morning will be here soon enough."

"Worry not, dear friend. I will be by in the morning with a riddle to split your mind," Zippy said with a smile.

She left, and Zippy played a few more songs before retiring to his chambers to feed his sort-of pet, Pumpkin. Though he loved his cat and little room, he knew this would not last forever. He was the lonely traveler and always had been. The restlessness in him never allowed him to rest for long. As he petted Pumpkin's long orange fur, he stared into the night, once again wondering where his hat would lie next.

Chapter 3

THE BLACKSMITH

As Razil descended the stairs, she stuffed the last morsel of bread her aunt had left on a plate outside her door into her mouth. It was buttery and practically melted on her tongue. She loved her aunt's baking almost more than beer.

Her aunt and uncle used to work the smithy; however, with age and their son choosing knighthood over taking over their business, they had hired Razil and Dessbelle as their successors. Razil handled most of the weaponry, while Dessbelle focused on armor and other trinkets. She had an affinity for tedious tasks that Razil could not match. Razil was happy for it, though sometimes the slow monotony of working at the blacksmith shop was too much to bear. Thus, last night's transgressions.

Razil could feel the heat radiating from downstairs, which meant Dessbelle was already hard at work. Her suspicions were confirmed as she slinked down the steps, and the corner of the room revealed a large messy bun of black hair. Razil slowed, knowing Dessbelle would chastise her for being late. She stopped just before entering the room, steeling herself for what was to come. She took a deep breath through her nostrils and let it out slowly. This shame was her own, and Dessbelle poking fun was not the problem; her self-judgment was.

Razil logically knew that Dessbelle's chastisement was that of a concerned older sister and not meant to hurt Razil's feelings. But Razil sometimes took her good-natured banter to heart, even if that wasn't its intent. Eventually, she got over herself and entered the room.

Dessbelle's olive skin was already cloaked in sweat and soot as she pulled the red, string-like metal through the drawplate. None crafted chainmail as Dessbelle did, and she never let Razil forget it. Dessbelle looked up from her task and cracked a smile as she said, "Good to see you rose from your chambers. I'm surprised you're not soaked in water from head to toe from your aunt or uncle waking you. Another minute, and it might have been me throwing ice water on you."

"They've softened with age. They often let me sleep in until after sunrise. Even give me breakfast," Razil said with a forced chuckle.

"Are those bags under your eyes?" Dessbelle asked as she looked back down at her craft, careful not to make a mistake in her work.

Razil placed a self-conscious finger under her eye and immediately felt the puffiness. "I do not know of what you speak," she said, lying.

"So, I shouldn't expect any ladies to come down those stairs in the next few minutes?" Dessbelle asked.

Razil choked on her spit. She quickly realized this made her sound guilty as Dessbelle looked up with an arched eyebrow and a mischievous grin. Razil was not naturally a flirt and often kept to herself; however, she could not deny the allure her quiet confidence seemed to have with many women in Gar Thanik. Usually, she would be mortified at the accusation, but Dessbelle was like a safe older sibling, and her teasing was friendly this morning. It lacked any real bite that it sometimes held.

"I assure you, no such thing transpired last night... Unfortunately."

With this, they both laughed. Their banter was interrupted by the creaking of the wooden doorway. Zippy walked through with his green doublet shining in the sunlight and his rosy cheeks pulled into a jolly smile. He clapped his pale hands and rubbed them together excitedly. "Are you ready for your morning riddle?"

"Ready as I'll ever be," Dessbelle said with amusement.

Zippy turned to face Razil. Though the necklaces she wore were hidden by the relatively high collar of the tunic she was wearing, they felt hot against her skin as Zippy stared at her. Every movement of the new necklace that swayed and tangled against her normal amulet felt like an accusation. She turned away from him, pretending to admire Dessbelle's craft.

"My ears are yours, Zippy," Razil said coolly.

Zippy tore his green hat from his bright red hair and danced a little jig, his gold rabbit medallion banging against his chest as he did. Zippy was often overtaken with excitement in the mornings. He skipped closer to Razil and Dessbelle, his voice ringing as he said, "When I am alive, my beauty is an envy. To some, I even draw blood. In death, I wilt and wither, no longer a sign of love."

Razil's brain was still fuzzy from the adrenaline left over from the night before. Normally able to guess Zippy's riddles quickly, she paused, causing Zippy to shake with excitement. She looked at Dessbelle, who looked perplexed as usual. She would be of no help.

Razil paced and thought, but was drawing a blank. The heat from the forge radiated over her, and she pulled up her sleeves, revealing her tanned and scarred forearm. She rarely showed her arms. There was one scar in particular she preferred to keep hidden, but she was in the company of those she trusted.

"Stumped, are we?" Zippy asked, bouncing on his toes.

Razil placed her hand on her chin, lost in thought. She turned her back to Zippy, avoiding his cheery hazel eyes, scrutinizing her every move. Dessbelle repeated the riddle to herself in a murmur, not helping Razil's concentration.

Her thoughts were interrupted by a husky voice bursting through the front door, "A rose!"

"Correct," Zippy praised as he reached up to pat the massive man on the back.

Razil smiled at her dear friend's entrance, not even having to look at the door to know who it was. She could never mistake the deep, burly voice that still held the accent of his barbarian roots.

Dracklin Mortim.

He was large, with bronzed, bulging shoulders visible beneath his leather shoulder pads. His strong abdomen was exposed down to his belly button, where his traditional tan sarong, patterned with orange designs from his homeland, Raufstig, resided. He bounded across the room and embraced Razil in a hug that lifted her feet off the ground.

When he released her, Razil noticed the bruises and cuts covering most of his body, some fresh, others covered in bubbling scabs. Razil hid a cringe. She could not bring herself to witness his battles at the coliseum. Though he won his freedom with his blade and cunning, and she was proud of him for doing so, his continued fighting worried her.

"What brings you to my smithy, Drack?" Razil asked.

He flashed a toothy grin. "I busted up Beatrice, and I was hoping you could repair her," he said, removing his battleaxe from his back.

A thin fracture in the metal started in the curved blade and continued midway through the ax. Razil knew she could fix it, but decided to give Drack grief before doing so. "It seems Beatrice has seen better days, good friend. Perhaps this is the sign you need to hang your hat in the gladiator arena after all."

"Pahhh! Nonsense. Beatrice still has the fighting spirit kicking in her. I know you can fix her and bring her back to her full glory, Razil," Drack said as he raised his eyebrows and pouted his bottom lip, which poked out through his short brown beard.

"Do you still have the fighting spirit flowing through you, though? You are aware you're free from Henworks and no longer have to fight in that bloody arena?" Razil asked as she met Dracklin's dark eyes. He shook his wavy hair back from his face and set his jaw.

"I am aware I am one of the richest men in Gar Thanik. That is because I fight in that 'bloody arena' you speak of. I can never return to Raufstig. You know that being taken captive is the greatest dishonor of my people. So, let me have my glory here and please fix my battleaxe."

Razil stared at Dracklin for several seconds, pondering his words and feeling sympathy in her gut. She knew who he was because, in a sense, they were the same. Gar was the greatest human-established country in Varki. Well, at least according to Gar. Sharkstown and Leedbriar may have differing opinions.

Gar was divided into three established territories, each with a city and an elected councilor. Gar Thanik was the largest of the cities and where the king resided, along with its elected official, Genna Landcaster. Though the elected officials of each area had political sway, the king was the final voice and ruled over all three cities, making it the capital of Gar.

To the north was Gar Hocklin, which was known for its horses and higher education. Only the wealthiest could afford to live or send their children to be schooled there. Gar Bladesin was the furthest south, and its primary purpose was to serve as a military stronghold and intimidate Gar's two southern rivals: the orcs and barbarians.

Barbarian raids were frequent, which was how many were captured and later used as slaves in Gar Thanik. That was Dracklin's fate.

Though Razil was never taken into custody and forced to fight in the gladiator arena to satisfy the bloodlust left over from the Orc Wars, she felt as if she knew this pain. She had been raised in the Dim District of Gar Thanik, where people were forgotten and left to rot in their hunger. She had no choice but to join a vicious thieves' guild as a child, only later to escape. In this way, she understood Drack; both of them were robbed of their chance of normalcy. Even though neither was forced to live that way anymore, the scars left behind never really healed.

Zippy stared at her awkwardly, not liking the tension. She realized she could not stop Drack from being Drack any more than Zippy could stop her from being herself. Though she wished desperately to live in a world where there was no Dim District and humans weren't used as pawns for deadly sport, that wasn't where she lived. She lived in Gar Thanik, a massive city and thriving metropolis for some and the death of others. She had no power to leave.

This smithy was the only thing keeping her fed and taken care of. She already knew what happened to her without it; she was a beggar, then a killer for a thieves' guild. Truthfully, she knew Dracklin had no power to leave either; he was stuck here, banished by Raufstig at his capture, and fighting was his only real skill.

"Give it here, you brute," Razil said as she extended her hand.

A smile spread across Drack's face, reaching his eyes as he handed it over. His ax was massive, given the giant size of his shoulders and arms, not to mention his overall domineering height. Luckily, Razil's forearms were strong from her endless hours in the forge, or Drack's battleaxe would have ended up on the ground.

"With that, I will leave you to it," Drack said with a wink as he made his way to the door.

"Dracklin, wait for me. I am bored and want to join whatever you have planned," Zippy interjected as he skipped to Drack's side.

"Of course, you do," Drack said with sarcasm dripping in his tone as he held the door open for their jolly gnomish friend. There were very few gnomes in Gar Thanik; most kept to themselves, making pies, but Zippy was the exception. He loved tagging along with his human friends.

"Bye, Drack and Zippy," Dessbelle shouted from the back, her eyes still on her craft.

Razil made her way to the center of the room where the stone forge resided. She began fanning the bellow to intensify the heat before placing the metal battleaxe in it. Fortunately, the breeze from the open windows was moving and keeping her cool as sweat began forming down her back.

She placed the ax in the forge and heated the metal until it turned a vibrant orange-red. Razil pulled it from the heat and placed it on the anvil to begin making quick work of banging out the fissure and returning the blade to its former splendor. Her forearms burned, but in a way that felt good. The work cleared her mind, but guilt began to creep into her heart as she felt the stolen necklace sticking to the sweat on her chest. She pushed the feeling aside and continued her work.

She finished mending the crack with exhausted forearms and sweaty palms. Even though she felt the blade was repaired, something seemed to be missing in Beatrice. The steel was from Gar, but its wielder was not. Something in the soul of the weapon was missing.

Razil grabbed her engraving tools from the back wall and began her work. There was a saying in Drack's home language, *gaasah malav krembar,* that stuck with Razil. It roughly meant, "Blood spilled grows the grass from the ground."

She began engraving the saying along the blade, along with the image of a pack of wolves running along the blade's edge and into the center. Drack's people worshiped the wolf, and their society operated similarly to a pack. She became obsessed with her craftsmanship and barely took a break for water. Hours passed until night fell, and finally, Razil felt satisfied. This was a blade that held the spirit of Dracklin Mortim.

Razil twisted from side to side and put a hand to her sweat-stained neck to try and rub away some of the tension she had not realized had built up there, stretching her stiff limbs toward the ceiling. The night air pushed through the window, soothing her hot skin.

Razil walked outside, taking in gulps of fresh air that entered her lungs and rejuvenated her spirit. Her body was spent, but her mind felt alive. She forgot how invigorated metalworking could make her feel when she let herself be creative. She closed her eyes and took in the sounds of crickets and frogs chirping away into the spring breeze.

Her serenity did not last.

In a whir, her vision was gone. Itchy fabric constricted around her face. She tried to break free, thrashing as hard as she could. Someone who smelled of old cheese and stale beer held her in place. She began kicking her legs, but it was in vain. Something in the fabric covering was blocking out her senses. Her body became limp, and her mind went fuzzy until consciousness left her body.

CHAPTER 4

A GAME OF QUESTIONS

Razil's arms were tied behind her back with a thick rope that chafed her skin as she tried to fight against it. She was tied to a rickety chair, itchy fabric obscuring her vision, and her mouth bound by cloth. She could still feel her favorite necklace pressed against her clammy skin and felt solace that her protection amulet had not been detected or stolen. The other necklace, the hideous one, had vanished.

Her immediate thoughts went to Wolf. She knew he could go back on his word and try to bring her back to his thieves' guild. It had been years since she'd escaped his grasp, and though he tried to bring her back forcibly, he was never successful and lost many henchmen in the process.

Razil had her protection amulet to thank for that. It was her curse wrapped in blessing. She'd obtained it during the night of her greatest regret, the catalyst that sparked her leaving Wolf once and for all. Wolf wanted the amulet that night; it was why they were there. He ordered Razil to remove it, and when she did, it felt as if every nerve ending in her arm was on fire. Her fingers felt like burned ash as she dropped the amulet and shoved her saber into the man's throat to kill him.

Wolf tried to take the amulet for himself, but it physically burned him as he attempted to grab it from the ground. Little did he know that the necklace had called to Razil like a siren song after she killed its bearer. She believed the amulet claimed her as its next owner—something Wolf realized too late.

When his back was turned that night, Razil slipped it into her pocket and had worn it ever since. Though the necklace freed her from Wolf's grasp, the lifeless look in the eyes of the innocent knight she had murdered would haunt her dreams for the rest of her life.

Wolf did not take Razil leaving well, but she could not continue working for a man who killed senselessly. After she left, several rogues tried killing her in her sleep, but something in the amulet always seemed to keep death at bay. Even the deepest wounds healed before eternal slumber could take her. She still did not know the extent of her amulet's powers, but she knew enough to keep her alive from even Wolf's most skilled killers.

Eventually, Wolf quit sending his people after her. She assumed he grew weary of losing rogues and made a truce with her to stay off his territory in exchange for her freedom. So, she left The Wolf's Teeth.

Around the same time, her aunt and uncle, desperate to retire, reached out to her regarding a different way to make a living. Though she still provided for her mom financially with what she earned as a blacksmith, she left the Dim District and her mother's home to work and live in the East End. All seemed well in her new life, and Wolf had left her alone after their last encounter. But men like Wolf rarely kept their word.

A harsh rip in the fabric covering her head revealed a weakly lit room and the large man who had taken her earlier. She identified him by his putrid smell. His face was pale and stern, and he held a short sword to her neck. The odor of old cheese and sweat was overwhelming, and part of her wished the bag was back on her head so she would no longer have to smell or see the unsightly man.

"So, what is the meaning of this? Let me guess, you're one of Wolf's rogues?" Razil asked. A brief sensation of fear churned her stomach. Razil knew that in the presence of one of Wolf's hired hands, she would have to be ruthless. If he could withstand the pain and remove her amulet, she would be vulnerable to dying.

The man only grunted in reply.

"Talkative," Razil retorted with disdain.

Razil scanned the room, careful not to cut herself on the blade against her neck. The room had stone walls with wooden support beams running along the ceiling. The floors were worn and splintered, matching the overall outdated and dilapidated room. In the corner was a straw cot, and Razil thought it curious that she was being held in someone's living chambers. She was not in Wolf's lair, bringing more questions than answers. Her observations were cut short by an annoying sound.

A shrill voice echoed from the corner of the room. "It is not Wolf and his thugs you should be concerned with, Razil. I am the leader of The Horned Lamb. I will bring Wolf and all of his rogues to their knees." The woman appeared in front of Razil in a dark green cloak with the hood pulled down. Her hair was in twists, and her skin was an umber tone with freckles that danced across her nose. Her irritated eyes burned into Razil's.

"The Horned Lamb?" Razil asked in a mocking tone, arching her eyebrows.

"Do not get a tone with me, Wolf's thug! You think I do not recognize you. You used to work very closely with him, then vanished into your new life. You think those in our field do not remember the right hand of the dreadful Wolf?" the woman yelled.

"You are correct. I once worked as Wolf's right hand, but that time is long gone," Razil said.

The woman removed an ugly necklace from her pocket and dangled it like a cat holding its prey. "It seems you think I am a fool. Wolf is the only one bold enough to steal from a Landcaster. She hired me to hunt you down, and you were not hard to find. Not many have a scar on their forearm as you do. Just because you carved out your marking does not mean you are no longer Wolf's."

Alyssandra must have seen her scar when she'd pulled the glove off Razil's hand. As the woman dangled the necklace more aggressively in Razil's face, three black dots imprinted on her wrist became visible. Razil smirked and said, "I thought I recognized you, Theona Martcrade. You sure have grown up. It seems you're the one working for Wolf, or perhaps you are working for the rumored rival who has snatched you from his grasp. I heard another thieves' guild was trying to take down The Wolf's Teeth."

Theona's eyes darkened in anger as she spat, "I already told you. You are not listening! I am the leader of The Horned Lamb! You should fear me, Razil Morganth."

"You are no leader. I remember you. You're a skilled rogue, Theona, but you did not orchestrate this." Razil scrunched her eyebrows together in realization. "It is Alyssandra Landcaster, is it not? She was awfully stealthy and versed in the art of the blade the other night. But why? What does a wealthy daughter of Gar Thanik's councilor need to start a thieves' guild for?"

At her last sentence, the bookshelf on the far side of the room creaked open, and Alyssandra Landcaster herself sauntered through. Her long hair was pulled back, and she no longer wore the clothing of a politician. Instead, she wore a long black cloak that covered her crimson shirt and black breeches tucked into knee-high boots.

Razil turned her head drastically to make more direct eye contact but was halted by the blade of Alyssandra's stinky henchman still snug against her neck.

Alyssandra's voice rang cooly in Razil's ears as she circled her seat, "Careful now, I would not wish your blood to stain the floor. So, you figured out that Theona is not the leader of The Horned Lamb. Bravo." Alyssandra clapped her hands together sardonically. "So, Razil, I will ask you directly. Does Wolf know I am the leader of The Horned Lamb? Did he send you to try and deter me?"

"I already told Theona. I do not work for Wolf. What is your obsession with The Wolf's Teeth? A bit extreme to start a rogue faction in direct competition with the richest man in Gar Thanik."

"I will ask the questions. What were you doing in my bedchambers, and what does Wolf know?" Alyssandra asked, her tone growing impatient.

"I heard Yurenda was no longer your lover, and I thought you might want company," Razil said with a smirk, masking a blush on her cheeks.

Alyssandra's cheeks reddened, and her shoulders tensed. She parted her lips just enough for Razil to see the small gap in her front teeth. She pinched her lips shut, letting the redness of her features pass before speaking again. She looked Razil up and down like a predator eying its prey. "Kill her," she said in a cool voice.

Her henchman smiled, revealing a yellow-stained mouth with several missing teeth. He lifted the sword above his head dramatically and gave a short wink in Razil's direction.

"Wait!" Razil shouted as the blade started to fall toward her neck. Though she would likely live, it would still be painful—amulet or not.

Alyssandra put her hand up, and the man halted with a pout. "Have you come to your senses?"

"Yes, yes. I do work for Wolf, and he is onto you, Alyssandra," Razil lied as she stared straight into the woman's beautiful, dark eyes. Something swarmed in her stomach at the intensity of their eye contact, and Razil began to wonder if hate butterflies were a thing.

"What does Wolf want with my necklace?" Alyssandra looked at her with narrowed eyes.

Suddenly, it occurred to Razil that something was off. Alyssandra kept darting her gaze to the necklace in Theona's hands. There was something unique about it. That must have been why Razil was drawn to it, regardless of how ugly it was. A game this would become.

"It is a special necklace, is it not?" Razil asked with a smile.

"No more special than any other. So why this one, Razil?" Alyssandra asked. The pitch in Alyssandra's voice slightly increased, and her eyebrow twitched. She was not a proficient liar.

"We both know that is not true. Is it, Lyss? Can I call you Lyss?"

"You most certainly cannot," Alyssandra said, her cheeks reddening and fire burning through her icy tone.

"Lyss, here's the thing. You want to know what Wolf knows about your magic necklace, and I want to leave this dreadfully morbid bedchamber and torture room, so we both have something to gain here." Razil slowly tried to inch her way out of her bondage as she spoke.

Alyssandra huffed and pouted her thick lips in a way that made Razil sweat even more than she already was. "I grow tired of your games, you fool."

"I think you may like the game, or I would already be dead, Lyss," Razil said with a sly smile.

"Quit calling me Lyss! Your game has ended as well as your life."

"Then the information I hold dies with me," Razil responded casually, hoping the other woman would buy the bluff.

Alyssandra let out an exasperated huff and ran her fingers through her hair. Razil slowly loosened the rope on her wrists, her mind racing as she wondered what could be so special about the necklace that Alyssandra was worried Wolf knew about it. She was concerned enough that even with Razil's poor behavior and a bloodthirsty thug standing next to her, Alyssandra kept her alive. She put the thought out of her head and focused on her escape.

Left. Right. Left. Right.

Up. Down. Up. Down.

Razil worked her wrists, the rope chafing and peeling her skin. She timed each movement with the huffs and anguished profanities Alyssandra hurled at Theona in frustration. The henchman next to Razil raised his eyebrows, his focus on his boss as he watched her apprehensively.

Finally, Razil's left wrist began to bleed enough to cause a slippery consistency, and she managed to wriggle an arm free. She swung her fist like a hammer at the man's groin, and he doubled over in pain. She threw herself backward, hoping the impact of the fall would break the chair.

It did not.

Razil was on her back, still strapped to the chair with one free arm waving wildly in the air. The henchman recovered and lifted his blade to strike. Alyssandra lifted her palm to stop him.

"Kroll, no. She's mine," Alyssandra said as she stalked closer to Razil, pulling a jewel-encrusted dagger that resembled her ugly necklace from her hip.

Before Alyssandra could reach Razil, a loud thud interrupted her. The wooden door at the front of the room shook with the force of a bull smashing it. A second thud followed, creating cracks in the wood, and a brawny shoulder broke through with the third attempt. The shoulder disappeared and returned with a fourth smash, and Dracklin Mortim appeared in the doorway, followed by a very sweaty Zippy Redbeard holding his lute.

"Drack? Zippy?" Razil shouted from the ground.

"I told you she'd be here!" Zippy bellowed.

Drack drew his battleaxe, Beatrice, as he rushed into the room. Kroll bounded to meet him. Their blades smashed, and the clanging of metal filled the room. Theona rushed at Zippy, but he began playing a calming melody in her direction, and she stopped in a trance. Drool began to drip from Theona's mouth as her eyes glazed over.

Alyssandra ran to the center of the room, face twisted in her fury, leaning over and pressing her dagger to Razil's throat. She paused, a flicker of emotion in her eyes.

"Coward," Razil breathed.

"Excuse me?" Alyssandra asked, looking truly taken aback.

"You know killing me when I'm tied up is a coward's move as well as I. I suspect it is why you have not killed me yet. The small sliver of integrity in you cannot bring yourself to kill with such an unfair advantage. That, or you do find me charming after all," Razil added with a wink.

Alyssandra cut the rope binding her legs and remaining arm. She sheathed her dagger and motioned for Razil to approach. "Let's see what Wolf's vermin are made of."

"Still not one of Wolf's," Razil corrected as she approached her defensively with her fists held up in front of her. Blood dripped from her arm, but Razil ignored it, mentally preparing for the fight ahead.

Alyssandra got the first shot, quicker than Razil anticipated. Razil blocked with just enough time to keep her nose from being broken.

Razil countered but was thrown off balance by Drack being pushed into her as he blocked a swing from Kroll. Alyssandra used Razil's instability to bring her to the ground by driving her shoulder into Razil's abdomen.

Alyssandra wrapped her hands around Razil's neck, straddling Razil's abdomen as she strangled her. Razil began to see spots, and part of her started to fear. Though she doubted Kroll was strong enough to remove her protection amulet, Alyssandra was made of tougher stuff. If she realized the necklace was what was keeping Razil alive, she might be fierce enough to act.

Razil grasped at Alyssandra's arms with her sweaty, blood-stained hands. They were slippery and made gripping Alyssandra's forearms impossible. Razil saw Zippy out of the corner of her eye begin strumming at his lute more aggressively.

The music was loud, but did not affect Razil because of her protection amulet. Slowly, Alyssandra's grip loosened from around her neck. Her eyes lulled to a droopy satisfaction. Razil silently thanked Zippy for his lute.

Razil's limbs began to regain feeling as Alyssandra's grip loosened. Zippy's red hair danced around his head as sweat poured down his arms, playing with every ounce of his being. Alyssandra's grip weakened with each beat until Razil sat up and pushed Alyssandra off. As she did, a thunderous sound followed by a ground-shaking roar distracted her.

For a moment, Razil thought she imagined the shaking due to oxygen deprivation. But Razil looked around to see everyone in the room no longer fighting, their attention fixed above them. Time seemed to stop. Everyone's jaws went slack as they stared at each other and then back at the ceiling in horrid anticipation. Razil could hear her heartbeat in her ears.

The entire room shook and became hotter as another roar rang in her ears. Everyone's eyes darted around the room in terror, hoping the sound was in their imagination. The room got hotter still, shaking once again. Everyone winced, and Kroll fell to his knees, cowering. The shrieks of townspeople could be heard coming from outside.

"What's going on?" Theona yelled.

"I'm unsure, but we must put aside this dispute and escape. Where are we? We need to work together. I fear we have a common enemy overhead," Zippy interjected with fear in his eyes.

Alyssandra paused. Turbulence was clear in her eyes as she pinched her lips together.

Zippy pulled on the sleeve of Alyssandra's cloak. "We will die if we do not act. Put your petty squabble aside."

The room shook again. Screams bellowed from above as a fire-like heat scorched through the room. The air was thick and unbreathable. Kroll coughed and wheezed, almost dropping his sword. Alyssandra's eyes set as turmoil was replaced by determination.

"Something is terribly wrong. I can feel it. We are in the basement, tucked beneath the councilor's meeting room. I can only hope my mother is still in the castle," Alyssandra said just loud enough to be heard. The ferocious wind in her sails from before all but snuffed.

"It keeps getting hotter. I fear there is a fire above. We must make haste!" Drack roared.

Razil stood to her feet, looking side to side. Though Razil had figured out quite a few of her protection amulet's abilities, she was unsure if she was fire-resistant. She pushed down the panic and looked at Zippy. He seemed to know something, and her musical little friend just might have the life experience to get them out of this mess. Or at least she hoped.

CHAPTER 5

THE FOE OF MY FOE IS A FOE

Something in Zippy stirred at Dracklin's words. He knew that sound. He had been alive much longer than these humans and had heard roars this mighty before. This was not just any creature. This was a dragon.

Zippy had only seen a gold dragon once outside of Leedbriar. He remembered how the wizards there were friends with the gold dragons of the Briar Forest. His brow furrowed as he glanced upwards, then shook his head slightly. No, it wasn't likely that this was an attack from the gold dragons and their wizard companions. The wizards of Leedbriar sought peace above all else.

This was something else altogether. Something sinister. He could feel the evil presence from the tip of his nose to the toenail of his big toe.

"Is there a way to escape this basement without surfacing? I fear we may face an enemy greater than we are ready to conquer," Zippy said, trying to remain calm even though his armpits were sweating through his tunic.

Alyssandra looked side to side before landing on a knowing look as a flicker of understanding settled in the brown depths of her eyes. Still, she said nothing, her fixed jaw and knowing eyes harboring a secret. A roar from above caused her bottom lip to tremble. Seconds felt like hours, and soon they would be dead if they did not move.

"We have no time for secrecy! This is a matter of life or death. A foe of my foe is a foe. And I can assure you this foe is larger than the three of us," Zippy sputtered through his teeth.

Alyssandra took a deep breath and sighed reluctantly. "There is a secret tunnel that leads from here to the castle. Its connection was to be used for the royals' escape from the castle only in the event of an insurrection. It is highly prohibited to use it in reverse."

The dragon's roar grew louder as the ceiling loosened with fire and debris above them.

Razil's eyes widened in horror as she pointed upward. The ceiling splintered and cracked like a vase dropped on the ground. The sturdy structure fractured as easily as ceramic as a massive claw ripped through the cracks, the black nail glinting in the dim light. Wood fragmented around them, and Zippy's heart lurched in his chest.

"Dragon!" Theona yelled in disbelief.

Urine streaked down the already foul henchman, Kroll, as he screamed in horror.

"Follow me," Alyssandra directed in a monotone voice. Shock covered her features, but she burst into action, running towards a bookshelf at the far end of the room. She shifted books in the middle of the shelf and exposed a veiled knob. Twisting the hidden knob, she revealed a secret entrance to a tunnel. She darted through the entrance as the room began to cave in.

Everyone followed suit, running as fast as their legs could take them. Zippy tried to keep up, but his limbs were not meant for this pace.

The further the gap grew between him and his friends, the more Zippy began to panic. For the first time, he may be the one to get left behind. He stopped the heat overwhelming, and his body exhausted.

Razil turned, seeing him falling behind. She ran towards him and threw him over her shoulder before spinning around to chase after the others. His stomach swooped in relief.

Zippy clutched his lute as tightly as his fingers could, careful not to drop it in the chaos. He bobbed like a child as he sagged across Razil's shoulders while she ran through dark puddles on the tunnel's floor until they reached the end, marked by a large oval door bolted shut. It seemed the only way to open it would be from the other side or by using a shaft key on this end.

"Do you have the key?" Zippy squeaked from Razil's shoulder.

Alyssandra shook her head, the life leaving her previously feisty eyes. Razil placed a hand on Alyssandra's shoulder in an instinctive empathetic gesture that earned a strange glare from Kroll and Theona.

"Help me, you dumb brute," Dracklin barked at Kroll as he began kicking at the locked door. It shook, but it did not give as the two men pounded it with their feet and shoulders.

The dragon roared from above, its vibrations shaking the tunnel ceiling. Debris continued to fall like snow from the ceiling, covering him in ash and wood shavings. Heat threatened to consume them all, as fire licked through the tunnel's disintegrating ceiling. The dragon seemed to be on a mission, and they were its priority.

Still, Zippy wondered how the dragon seemed to know where they were. He did not understand why their group was of interest when many tasty townspeople were surely visible roaming the streets. Before he could ponder it further, another wave of flames burst through the wood overhead. Zippy's brow began to drip sweat onto Razil's shirt.

He did not know if she was even aware she was still holding him as she began pacing.

Theona and Alyssandra joined the men beating at the door. The door began to buckle as it creaked against its hinges. Zippy could only watch. Breaking things was not his forte. He had never felt more helpless as he rested on Razil, hoping they would make it out of this affair alive. The door fell flat with a loud crash as the next wave of flames burst through the ceiling.

Dust filled the air and clouded Zippy's vision as he felt them running through another dark tunnel, which led deeper into the ground as descending steps were revealed. Nothing could be seen in the lightless tunnel, and the only sound was the scurrying of rats and the loud pants of the running humans he was trapped with.

The tunnel seemed to go on forever, even though the castle was a stone's throw from the councilor's headquarters. Time seemed to pass slower than usual. Fear filled him. He was not ready to die. He had more songs to write and more places to see. He felt Razil moving up and realized the stairs changed course, and they must be moving closer to the castle.

"We're here!" Drack shouted over his shoulder.

He burst through the door like the brute he was. Zippy's eyes had adjusted to the dimness, so the sudden light from the torch-lit room caused him to squint. Razil still held Zippy like a child. His group let out a collective sigh of relief to be out of the tunnel.

"Dear friend, you may let me down now," Zippy said as he lightly tapped Razil's shoulder.

"Right, sorry," she said as she lowered him to his feet.

When his feet were firmly against the ground, Zippy realized they were not alone. King Gunthar Luvian and his family, along with Councilor Genna Landcaster, were also there.

The king and his wife, Edid, were having a heated conversation while Genna sat with the two princesses, who were huddled on the ground, looking terrified. They clutched their dolls as the muffled roars of a dragon could be heard through the stone walls. The ground shook with each movement of the creature, causing the whole room to seemingly hold its breath at the horrors to come.

The king turned to look at the intruders. "Alyssandra! Thank the heavens you have survived. We saw the councilor's headquarters being taken by the dragon, and we fled to the castle cellars."

At the sound of Alyssandra's name, Genna looked up. She jumped to her feet and wrapped Alyssandra in a tight squeeze. Her dark brown hair with greying streaks brushed against her daughter's shoulders, and her crinkled eyes spilled tears. When her mother released Alyssandra from their embrace, she stepped back, peering over Alyssandra's shoulder with a perplexed expression.

"Who are these people, my daughter?" Councilor Landcaster asked.

Alyssandra's eyes widened. "They are friends of mine. I met them at the gladiator match the other night before I retired early. They came over for afternoon tea."

Zippy tapped his foot and stared at her in disbelief. Was her mother going to believe this lie? Razil did not refute the statement, and neither did Dracklin, which surprised Zippy. Zippy realized the truth would only endanger them further and decided to go along with the façade.

"King Luvian and Councilor Landcaster, I am Zippy Redbeard. A pleasure to make your acquaintance. I do appreciate your hospitality amidst the dire circumstances in this lovely cellar." At the end of his sentence, Zippy bowed at his waist and removed his cap. Drack, Razil, Theona, and Kroll followed suit.

"Any friend of my daughter is welcome," Genna said, her kind eyes wrinkling further.

"Hogwash," said a brash voice from the corner of the room. A large, pale man with a bald head and a greying blond beard stalked towards them. "This is a haven for royalty and governing officials in the case of an emergency. This space is not meant for civilian eyes. Do something, brother!"

The king put out his palm. "Viron, enough. This is not a normal uprising of the townsfolk. This is a dragon. These people may stay. But I must go. The dragon is here for a purpose, and I will not cower while it devours our city."

Edid Luvian placed her hands in her husband's wavy greying hair. She pulled him to look in her eyes and said, "Please do not do this. Our girls need you, Gunthar."

A loud clamoring from above, followed by the roar of a dragon, filled the room. Zippy clutched his hat tightly in his hands, fear ripping through every morsel of his tiny being.

"I wish to speak to the king." The bellowed words seemed to vibrate through the castle walls.

The king backed away from his wife and whispered, "I love you." He pulled a sword from his hip and ascended the cellar stairs.

Razil followed him, and Zippy could not believe his eyes. "Razil Morganth, get back here."

She did not look back even as Zippy tried to play a quick tune in her direction to lure her back. That blasted protection amulet. Reluctantly, Zippy scurried behind her, hearing Dracklin on his heels.

"Razil, what are you doing?" Zippy hissed.

"I want to see the dragon. If we are all to die, I refuse for it to be in a cellar while being burned to a crisp," she whispered.

"I agree," Dracklin chimed in. He pulled Beatrice from his back and handed Razil a dagger from his hip to defend herself.

The king did not look back or join the conversation. He seemed indifferent about the strangers following him. The dragon was his only focus. His steps were steady, but Zippy could sense his fear. After his many years walking Varki's mortal plane, Zippy had become gifted at sensing what others felt.

The king halted at the top of the steps and took a deep breath before opening the wooden door. Zippy's stomach swirled in anticipation. The dragon he had seen in the past terrified him with its massive structure, and it was of good character. He could not imagine what horror the evil dragon would inflict. The king walked through the door and into the great room, followed by the steady steps of Razil and Dracklin. Both of them were trained fighters, but the slight quiver in their jaws showed Zippy neither of them had faced a foe of this magnitude. With trembling legs and rumbling bowels, Zippy followed his friends.

The great room still stood, the stone walls unyielding though the windows were broken and the king's throne was ablaze. Still, King Luvian was undeterred as he walked towards the burning wooden doors that several knights were trying to extinguish with water buckets. King Luvian kicked through the burning door, and Razil and Dracklin followed with weapons ready. Zippy sent a quick prayer to Zajac, rubbing the rabbit medallion around his neck that bore Zajac's image. Though he was not devout, he hoped Zajac would look past this fact and protect him on this quest.

Zippy jumped through the door, the crackle of flames and screams assaulting his ears. Smoke filled his lungs, and his vision was obscured momentarily by the chaotic swarm of townspeople as they scurried and fled for their lives.

"Come forth, dragon! It is I, King Gunthar Luvian. Reveal yourself, you wretched beast," the king yelled into the sky with a puffed-out chest.

A strong wind swept around Zippy, removing his hat. The swooshing sound became louder and louder until a red dragon appeared, lowering in front of the king. Inadvertently, Zippy fell to his bottom and scrambled backward.

Its dark red scales bulged sharply from its skin, and smoke billowed from its nose. Its eyes were a snake-like yellow with slits pulled tight with vitriol. Its tail slammed into the cobbled road, cracking the ground with such force that even Dracklin's knees buckled.

"Ahh, the cowardly king at last. I am surprised to see the Luvian line has lasted this long. I am Crimshyrbane, and you will bow before me," the dragon bellowed.

"My ancestors defeated yours, did they not, Crimshyrbane? I bow before no one," the king said through gritted teeth.

Crimshyrbane turned his head haphazardly and released a flame from his jowls that burned at least twenty townsfolk. His piercing teeth were covered in soot as he turned to face them once more.

The king yelled and rushed the dragon, but Crimshyrbane released a flame that stopped just short of burning the king. "I have your attention, do I now?" Crimshyrbane asked with curved lips.

"What do you want, dragon? Surely there is a reason you did not envelope me in your flame," King Luvian shouted.

"Come to your senses, I see. What I want is very simple. The land of my ancestors. And all of the gold you have hidden within the city as well as the dragon blade. I could rip the city to shreds in search of what I seek, killing all who roam its pathetic streets. But that, my dear king, would be quite cumbersome. I can smell the weapon and gold throughout the streets, but it is hidden from my view. Leave my desired items piled in the city's center, and vacate within forty days. This is the only way you shall be spared. Generous of me, is it not?" Crimshyrbane threw his massive head back and laughed. Small flames dripped from his lips, and smoke puffed in little spurts from his nose.

"And if we do not?" King Luvian asked.

"Then you shall watch your city burn and your people with it."

"I do not know of the hidden items you seek."

"Do not play stupid with me, King. I can smell it. Leave it for me in plain sight. Vacate the city. You have forty days. Rest assured, I will return to claim my homeland. Your ancestor's crusade ends now. Five hundred years do not erase the memories of the evils of your people. I am the last of my kind because of those monsters, and I will reclaim the land and its spoils, which are rightfully mine." The dragon flapped his wings once more. The force caused Razil to fall to the ground near Zippy as the dragon disappeared into the smoke-filled sky.

CHAPTER 6

THE KING'S DECREE

Word from the king reached every household in Gar Thanik, and people from the Dim District all the way to the Nobles' District gathered on the castle's lawn. The smell of the dead burning outside the city filled Razil's nostrils as she looked at the despair in her neighbor's eyes. The councilor's headquarters lay in ruins next to the castle, which stood with broken windows and missing stones.

The aqueduct that flowed through the city center was filled with debris, and workers became drenched as they struggled to remove it. Ash flitted about and landed on Razil's clothing like a sick snow. The dragon's stain on the city was vast, and the people were in shambles as they awaited the king's statement.

Razil's arms burned from her work the night before. She couldn't sit still, couldn't sleep, couldn't deal with what happened. Something in the dragon stirred a part of her she didn't understand. She had this restless feeling in her that she sometimes felt when working at the smithy. So, she worked. She helped discard the dead, and her only reprieve was that her family and Dessbelle weren't among them.

"What do you think he is going to say?" Zippy asked as he rocked back and forth on his heel.

"Nothing good. Either we are going to war with the red dragon, or we are fleeing our land. It's not like we can procure the item he seeks. Dragon's blades are that of fiction," Dracklin replied. His stance was more solemn than normal, so Razil patted his shoulder to show support.

"Perhaps there will be good news. Who knows, maybe the king knows more about the fables of Gar's ancestral blades than we do. Surely, he will have a plan to face the dragon," Zippy said as he looked up at them.

Razil nodded, and Dracklin shrugged his shoulders. She loved Zippy's positive attitude, but it was hard to shake how bleak things felt.

From the corner of her eye, Razil noticed Alyssandra Landcaster standing towards the front of the crowd. She turned and caught Razil's eye. She looked as broken as she did angry. Razil had been wrong about her. She was more than just an entitled daughter of a councilwoman.

Razil smiled in her direction, and she was met with a scowl before Alyssandra turned to face the castle once more. Razil had hoped the dragon encounter would have made her theft of Alyssandra's ugly necklace water under the bridge, but to her disappointment, it had not.

"She's a rotten batch," Drack said as he followed Razil's line of sight.

"Yes, indeed," Razil replied, shifting her eyes to the side. Truth be told, she did not find Lyss rotten at all. She was intrigued by her if nothing else.

"Rotten is a bit on the harsh side," Zippy chimed in as he twisted his long red beard in his fingers.

"All the egregiously rich are rotten," Drack replied under his breath as he crossed his burly arms.

Razil found the comment odd given Drack's profits since becoming a free fighter in the gladiator arena. The conversation shifted when Razil saw her Uncle Tyrak and Aunt Gertrude from across the crowd. Razil waved her arms at them, and Uncle Tyrak's brown eyes twinkled as he recognized her. He shook Aunt Gertrude's arm, and she looked at Razil with relief. They walked over and pulled Razil into a hug. She allowed their comfort to seep into the edgy parts of her heart, thawing the ice that had formed in her veins at the dragon's encounter.

Her aunt's short study frame pulled back first, and she looked up to meet Razil's eyes. "Thank goodness you survived. We were worried when you did not return last night."

"I was helping to discard the dead. Sorry I gave you a scare," Razil said with guilt pitting in her stomach. Just because she knew they were safe, given the absence of their carcasses, didn't mean she shouldn't have checked in. She knew better. Though they were vacant in her childhood, her aunt and uncle stepped up in a big way when she matured to adulthood. She owed them more than this being their first encounter since the dragon's appearance.

Dracklin took Uncle Tyrak's strong, wrinkled hand. "Good man, glad to see you two made it."

"You as well, Dracklin and Zippy. I am hoping the dragon steers clear of Gar Bladesin. I worry for our son," Uncle Tyrak responded.

"Have either of you seen my mother?" Razil asked. As she asked, Dessbelle appeared behind her.

"I checked on Marisol this morning. She is alive and well... Perhaps, not so well, but not from the dragon," Dessbelle said as she awkwardly pulled at her thick black bun.

Razil knew this was Dessbelle's way of telling her that her mother was either drunk or hungover. The news did not surprise Razil. It did not take much to tip the bottle in her mother's hand. The scare of a dragon was enough to send her into a bender for days.

Aunt Gertrude pulled on Razil's sleeve. "I will check on my sister later, love. Do not worry for her now."

Razil looked down and gave her aunt a haphazard smile. She knew she meant well, but Razil always worried about her mother. She distanced herself and did not interact with her often to protect her peace. Marisol's anger and drinking made it nearly impossible to have a relationship with her, but that did not stop the worry and the love she still had for her.

Their conversation was interrupted by a sudden, deafening silence. King Luvian and Queen Luvian appeared in the castle's doorway, followed by Councilor Landcaster. King Luvian stood tall with ash still remnant on his red doublet, and his golden crown rested assuredly on his mussed blond hair. He took steps to look his normal part, but the havoc from the previous day peeked through his attempted unfazed appearance. The wrinkles in his eyes seemed to have deepened overnight.

"People of Gar Thanik, we have survived the red dragon. Some of you may be wondering if we will surrender our lands. I will get straight to the point. I will not run from this land. My ancestors before me led the Red Dragon Crusades. Though the weapons of that age are lost, the heart is not. Each of you holds our ancestors' breath, and we will not leave Gar to the evil dragon," the king said as he addressed the crowd.

The crowd began murmuring. Fear of death escaped their lips as they gossiped with their fellow citizens.

King Luvian raised his arms and crossed them in the air. "Silence!" The king's words stopped the loose lips, and the crowd quieted again.

King Luvian shifted his crown and continued his speech. "I will send the brave people of Gar Thanik to vanquish this dragon as our ancestors did before us. I ask each of you to look inside yourself and question whether that might be you. Gar Thanik's archers and knights cannot be spared. We need them to defend the civilians lest the dragon return. However, if you have an adventuring heart with a fighting spirit, I ask you to take on this challenge. If you bring me Crimshyrbane's head, you will be rewarded with the southern portion of Gar Thanik's land to the East. The land will be established, and you will be named councilor and given legitimate rule as a city within our wonderful country, Gar. You will be regarded with equal authority in our sister city's Gar Hocklin and Gar Bladesin."

The crowd erupted in conversations, and the king could not silence them this time. Something in Razil stoked and turned. A fire lit in her spirit, and she knew she must go. This was her opportunity to build a community where people would not suffer as she did in her youth, as she fought and scavenged for the crumbs that rolled off the rich people's lips. This was her chance at a fresh start, and she would let no one take it from her. As these thoughts swirled through her mind, she saw Wolf in the crowd.

He had a sinister smile, and she knew his sentiments were the same. A man like him with that level of power would do the opposite. He would create a lawless town where he preyed on the weak for his own gain. She would not allow it.

Finally, the crowd quieted again as they waited for more information, the restless energy humming beneath the surface.

King Luvian puffed out his chest. "I have received word from Councilor Rett Dentwood of Gar Blacesin through my falcon this morning. A retired knight named Clinsel reportedly saw the dragon on its way to Gar Thanik. Information from him should be your first objective. If you wish to take this quest to slay the red dragon and claim your land, sign the decree placed within the tavern wall of The Red Dragon Inn with your name, along with any accompanying you under your command. From there, you shall receive official documentation marking you as an official soldier of the king on this quest."

Wolf was the first to break from the crowd. His stride was confident as he stalked towards The Red Dragon Inn, followed by several of his rogues. Razil knew he would bring some with him on his quest and leave others to keep an eye on Gar Thanik. Razil stomped after him towards the tavern.

"Where are you going?" Zippy questioned from behind her.

"To sign the king's decree," Razil answered.

"Not without us you aren't," Drack said as he grabbed Zippy by the doublet and pulled him along, causing Zippy's face to grow even paler than usual.

"This is a fool's quest. I am no warrior," Zippy pleaded. "Weren't you the one who said there was no such thing as a dragon's blade, Dracklin? How are we going to kill this thing?"

"Who cares. I'd follow Razil anywhere, and I have ached to fight out in the field as I did when I lived in Raufstig," Dracklin asserted.

Razil internally squirmed, knowing that Zippy was right. It was a fool's quest, but she could not stop herself. This was her chance to leave behind her past once and for all.

"Dracklin, watch after our niece. I know we cannot stop her, but I expect your battleaxe's support," Uncle Tyrak yelled and received a thumbs-up from Drack.

"Why do I feel I will not like this?" Zippy groaned.

"Nonsense, Gar Razil will be wonderful," Dracklin replied.

Razil smirked. She liked the sound of that. Gar Razil. A place where all good-intentioned people doing their best are welcome to contribute how they can—a place where none hunger and all have homes. Gar Razil would be the home she had always wished for.

CHAPTER 7

INTO THE FOREST WITH FRIENDS

Zippy shook his head from side to side, flinging the light mist off his red beard and back into the drizzling sky. The rain descending upon them was partially reduced by the broadleaf trees above. Their green leaves glistened, and birds squawked from their branches.

Zippy was happy to avoid the main road and take the path less traveled as they moved south through the Gar Forest. Firstly, the main road was dangerous. Most who signed up for the king's decree were criminals, and the forest gave their group some cover from the rest of those partaking in this quest. More importantly, the forest brought joy to Zippy and ignited his wandering spirit. And for the first time, he was not wandering alone.

Dracklin and Razil were mostly quiet as they navigated, except for the squishing of their boots as they trudged across the softening ground. Zippy did not mind the silence but decided to break it nonetheless.

"The dirt is my toil, but often I am at rest. My use is only as good as the hands wrapped around my breast."

Dracklin looked back, his dark wavy hair swaying as he did. "What in Varki's mortal plane, Zippy?"

"A shovel," Razil stated.

"Correct," Zippy cheered as he clapped his hands.

"No fair. You did not announce it was a riddle. I thought you'd been possessed," Dracklin said, pouting. The giant man looked silly when he frowned, like an oversized bear with a bad attitude.

"Do not fear, dear Dracklin. I have another up my sleeve," Zippy jested.

"Go on then," Dracklin muttered.

"Don't be such a sore loser, Drack," Razil said with a sly smile. She looked back at Zippy. "Let's hear it."

"With enough heat, I am translucent; otherwise, I am a mess. I sneak into your cheeks, chafing at best," Zippy said with a smile, amused at how his riddle caused Razil to stare into the sky in contemplation while Dracklin stroked his beard.

"Can we have another clue?" Razil asked with furrowed brows.

Zippy did a little side-step jig and removed his cap for theatrics. "No clue, I'm afraid."

Dracklin ripped his hand from his beard and turned to face Zippy. The glower previously in his dark eyes was replaced by merriment. "Sand!"

"Correct!"

"What? That is not fair. Dracklin was born in the desert. Of course he was going to guess sand," Razil said with a huff.

"Do not be such a sore loser," Dracklin said with a pat on Razil's shoulder.

Razil retaliated with a punch to his exposed stomach that ended in Dracklin pulling her into a headlock. When Razil's face turned such a bright red the freckles on her nose disappeared, she stomped hard on Dracklin's toe, causing him to drop her on the ground.

"Oh, please do not hurt each other," Zippy said with concern welling in his chest. His friends were very large and raucous.

"It is all in good fun," Dracklin said as he ruffled Razil's already messy blonde hair with his massive hand.

Razil pushed off his hand and pretended to fix her hair. "You are a foolish oaf of a man."

"Thank you," Dracklin replied with a bow.

Zippy decided against more riddles for fear of stirring the hornet's nest. Though he knew they loved each other, Dracklin and Razil were the most competitive humans he had ever met. Their sibling-like rivalry grew out of control under the best of circumstances. With the added stress of tracking a dragon, he feared it might combust and cause undue issues.

He was used to frequent wrestling matches and verbal sparring between the two back in Gar Thanik. However, the three of them had never been on an adventure like this together before. Frankly, Zippy had never been on an adventure with anyone before. Typically, his quests were solitary, and he was leaving to start somewhere fresh.

He looked at his friends and smiled. Though it was a change to have others travel with him, it was a welcome change. This surprised him, but he allowed the content feeling to settle in his chest. Maybe he could keep ties after all. Even as he thought it, the temporary relief was clouded by self-doubt. They were on a quest that would come to an end. Eventually, Zippy would be on his own again, even if he enjoyed the present company. He shook his head free of the thoughts and continued after his much larger friends.

They walked in relative silence. Zippy could sense apprehension in Razil. Her head seemed to be on a constant swivel. He recognized she was probably on the lookout for Wolf, who was surely also taking this path, although Zippy doubted he would attack. He had lost plenty of rogues to Razil in the past, and he would need all of the warm bodies he could muster to follow him if he planned to slay the dragon as they did.

When the sun began to fade, Dracklin stopped walking. "I think we should make camp for the night."

"We may need to forgo fire. It will alert others to our position," Razil said as she scanned their surroundings.

"Only a fool would attack the greatest gladiator of Gar Thanik," Dracklin said with a puffed-out chest, followed by a gag from Razil.

"Though Dracklin sounds pompous. I think he may have a point. An attack on us is a risk. Defeating a dragon is no easy feat, and losing members of their group so early would be unwise for any of our competitors," Zippy said with an encouraging smile in Razil's direction.

She only nodded in response and set her satchel with thief's tools down on the ground. She shifted her foraging pouch to the front of her belly and walked into the woods alone, her saber still on her hip. Dracklin began making a fire, and Zippy was impressed when it took, considering the dampness of the kindling. His barbarian roots proved helpful in times like this. Sweat poured down Dracklin's back as Zippy strummed his lute. The fire was soon ablaze and dancing merrily against the night sky.

Dracklin looked at Zippy and scoffed. "Thank you for all of your help with the fire."

"Oh, it is my pleasure. Glad the music was encouraging," Zippy said with an irrepressible grin.

Razil appeared from behind Zippy, startling him. She was so light on her feet that he often didn't hear her coming. "Sorry, Zippy. I didn't mean to scare you."

"All is well, dear friend," Zippy replied with a hand over his thundering heart.

"Please tell me you found something for us to eat," Dracklin said, his belly echoing his plea with a loud grumble.

Razil shoved her fists into her foraging pouch and pulled out two handfuls of large mushroom caps. She waggled her eyebrows. "Have I ever come empty-handed?"

"Give them here," Dracklin said, dark eyes beaming.

Dracklin grabbed the mushrooms like an excited child and roasted them on the fire. The smell of mushrooms cooking made Zippy's mouth water. He had not realized how hungry he was.

When Dracklin handed Zippy his steamed, slightly charred mushroom, he attempted to savor it but ended up devouring it in seconds. Razil and Dracklin ate even faster than he did, and Dracklin leaned back against the tree stump with his back and patted his stomach.

Zippy picked up his lute and began strumming. Dracklin tilted his head to look at Zippy and smiled as he rose to his feet and danced around the fire. Razil rolled her eyes at him. Dracklin simply extended his hand.

"Have a dance with me, friend," Dracklin insisted.

Razil reluctantly rose to her feet and began following the beat of Zippy's lute. Dracklin smiled and clapped as his feet bounced around the fire. Razil followed and a toothy grin took over as her freckled button nose scrunched and her eyes crinkled. Dracklin took a swig of what Zippy assumed was alcohol from a small bladder on his hip and extended it to Razil, who coughed violently after a small sip. The sight inspired a song that Zippy just couldn't keep in.

Licking, spitting in the air,
My feet flit around and around.
The dance of the fire's tongue,
Heating the very ground.
I dance, I drink, I sing,
But I do not have a care,
Because around this earnest fire,
Alcohol warms my belly hairs.

Razil and Dracklin clapped in Zippy's direction and warmth filled his chest as he stood to bow. Nothing made him happier than a song shared with friends.

"With that, I must leave you for a moment to get my bearings," Razil said, wiping the sweat from her brow.

"Do not be too long, friend," Zippy said in concern. He knew she needed to decompress from the day, but he still worried.

"I would not dare," Razil replied with a smile as she walked into the trees, the moonlight guiding her path.

This was usual for her. She would laugh during the day, answering Zippy's riddles, then at some point wander off to be alone even in Gar Thanik. Even though it was usual, Zippy still worried for her. They were not within city walls anymore, not that the Dim District Razil grew up in was any safer. He resolved to leave her to her peace and quiet for the time being.

Zippy strummed quietly as he and Dracklin sat in silence. He made it through six songs before he became troubled. "Do you think Razil is all right?"

"You know how she is," Dracklin replied with a shrug.

"I'm just going to poke around," Zippy said as he rose to his feet, lute in hand. He knew how she was, but it did not mean he would not check on her. Sometimes quiet friends need checking up on even if they do not admit it out loud.

He followed the soft indentations left by Razil's boots, his proximity to the ground helping him track in the darkness of night. He followed the footprints deep into the trees until he suddenly heard strained whispers coming from ahead.

"I know who you are, Razil Morganth. You used to be the right hand of Wolf. My patience is dwindling. What do you want with this necklace?"

"You're beautiful this time of night," Razil's voice carried quietly in the breeze.

Zippy's mind raced. He knew Razil's voice by heart, but who was the other woman? He peeked from behind a tree and saw Alyssandra Landcaster straddling Razil, holding a jewel-encrusted blade to her neck.

"Do not play games with me, Razil. I will slit your throat where you lie," Alyssandra said in a heated whisper.

Zippy's stomach lurched into his chest at the sight. Though he knew Razil had the protection amulet, seeing his friend beneath a blade was a jarring sight. He calmed his nerves and pulled his lute from his back. His friend needed him, and he knew what to do.

Zippy jumped from behind the tree where he hid and played a calming tune in Alyssandra's direction. Alyssandra rushed to her feet and stormed towards him. Her eyes were wild with fury.

"You again," she hissed, only to suddenly stop in her tracks and drop her weapon, which shone much like the necklace Razil had attempted to steal.

Razil got to her feet and brushed off her tunic calmly. She pulled the saber from her hip and pressed it to Alyssandra's back. "Where were we, love?" Razil asked with a smirk.

"I just want to know why you broke into my home and why you want this necklace. Why was it important enough to steal? I am afraid and backed into a corner. Wolf discovered my true identity as the leader of The Horned Lamb the night I signed the king's decree in the tavern. I should have known seeing me there with Theona would have tipped him off. I had to leave Kroll and Theona behind to protect my assets from the members of The Wolf's Teeth left behind. I am all alone, and all I know is the last person who stole a necklace from someone I loved was Wolf, and I want to know why you were in my bedroom the other night." Alyssandra admitted in her lullaby state. Her face flushed an embarrassed red after she spoke.

"Lyss, my darling. I have told you before. I do not work for Wolf anymore. The necklace was just for sport. I do not wish to cause your family harm. Now, please rid me of your company. We both seek to kill the dragon, and you have made the foolish decision to leave Theona and Kroll behind and go forward yourself on this quest. I am not your greatest threat. Save your energy for Wolf and Crimshyrbane," Razil said as she sheathed her saber and walked toward Zippy.

Zippy quit playing his music and looked at Alyssandra once Razil was on her way back to camp. Alyssandra looked lost and Zippy felt sympathy for her. Her eyes were hollow and haunted as she looked back at him.

"Razil may seem like the enemy, but she is not her past. She is too pure for the world she was thrust into. Good luck finding and slaying Crimshyrbane," Zippy said.

Alyssandra responded with an ashamed nod and turned on her heel to tread back into the trees.

CHAPTER 8

THE GOLDEN BOY OF GAR BLADESIN

The trip to Gar Bladesin had been relatively quiet after their encounter with Alyssandra, other than a dead caravan of five adventurers, surely on the same quest as them. By the looks of the knife wounds and the lack of supplies left on their persons, it was safe to say Wolf had killed and raided them along the way. He had a way of killing and taking what he wanted, according to Razil.

Zippy was just happy they had not been attacked by the likes of Wolf yet. He knew Wolf respected Razil and recognized her as a worthy combatant, but he was skeptical that this seeming peace would last. Someone like Wolf would confront them at some point, as he would any other group on this quest. He would want to make sure he was the only one standing at the end of this with the red dragon's head in his hands. However, Wolf was smart and the attack would not be at random. He would wait for the opportune time as not to lose too many of his own in the process.

The trees they walked through soon disappeared as they got closer to Gar Bladesin. It had been almost a week of fast-paced walking, and

Zippy was delighted to see a city again. Zippy knew they were here for information, but he also hoped a pint of beer was in his future.

As they approached Gar Bladesin, Razil pulled the king's sealed document from her pocket and placed it in the hands of the armored knight at the entrance gate. Zippy smiled at her as she looked over the parchment. Guards lined the large wooden walls, several standing in their watch tower with bows pulled taut. Apparently, Gar Bladesin had not seen friendly visitors of late.

After scanning the wrinkled parchment in her gloved hands, the guard looked at each of them. Her brown eyes were set on Zippy, who felt exhilarated at visiting the new city, never having had the chance to come here before.

"Wipe the smile off your face, gnome. I know the kind the king has decided for his dragon quest. He did not send the noble knights or archers within the country of Gar. Instead, he sent the rogues and scum off the streets." She gave a deep huff and continued, "You are welcome in the city with this document; however, any trouble from you lot and you'll be out of our city on your bum. There are other adventuring groups here. General Mattan and the knights of our town expect nothing but civility, though I know it is not easy for your kind."

Dracklin looked insulted as he raised his left arm, but Razil quickly swatted it down and cut him off before he had a chance to speak. "We will be on our best behavior. Where might we find Clinsel?"

The knight rolled her steely eyes and said, "He is normally whittling on the tavern's porch this time of day."

Zippy removed his cap and bowed. "Thank you, dear knight."

The knight muttered angrily under her breath and opened the wooden gate. It creaked in protest along with the knight's irritated huffs, revealing the military city from within. The very first sight when the gate opened was the barracks. Gar Thanik had a barracks as well but it was nothing compared to this.

The barracks stood three stories with a stone base and a large training yard. It had hefty windows on all three floors with metal bars overtop, and the wooden walls of the second and third stories had a waxy seal. On the roof were several guards standing tall next to the ballista. The grandeur of the structure gave Zippy the impression few would be brave enough to try and attack this city. Not that others had not tried. It was a sight for many battles won during the Orc Wars; however, orcs were known for ego over intelligence.

Knights in training sparred in the yard while officers yelled commands as the parrying of blades rang in the air. To the left of the massive structure, the whizzing of arrows buzzed like a swarm of bees as young archers practiced on straw targets. A bald, barrel-chested man with a maroon cape appeared in the barracks doorway. Zippy assumed he was General Krieger Mattan based on his regalia. The massive man nodded in Razil's direction, and she gave a small wave. Zippy looked at Razil for an explanation, but she avoided his gaze. He did not like the feeling he was being kept out of the loop but resigned to follow her in silence.

They walked through the militant city on their quest to find the tavern. Its cobbled roads were similar to Gar Thanik, but the buildings lining it were different. Gar Thanik was lively and full of shops and merchants. Entertainment spilled out from every corner of Gar Thanik, from the gladiator's coliseum to the variety of people performing and talking loudly as they walked the streets. Gar Bladesin, on the other hand, had rigid structures with very little color. The streets mostly consisted of knights walking tall and with a purpose, and that purpose did not include talking with outsiders.

When they approached The Tilted Tavern, its essence starkly contrasted with the barracks and other pristine structures. Its wooden walls had seen better days, with peeling maroon paint and a roof full of cracked and missing shingles. The hanging sign with the tavern's name was faded, and a musty smell emitted from the entrance. Several older men sat on the porch in squeaking rocking chairs.

"Do any of you go by the name Clinsel?" Dracklin asked as he glanced over the elderly men.

One of the elderly men rocking in the farthest chair raised his greying eyebrows. "What's it to you, barbarian?"

"We are on the quest to vanquish the red dragon, old man. The king sent us from Gar Thanik," Dracklin responded gruffly as he grit his teeth. Barbarian tribes and people who resided in any part of the country of Gar had always had a hostile relationship.

The elderly man grabbed some wood from his pocket and began shaving away with a whittler's knife. No one spoke on the porch for several long seconds, and the sound of shaved wood echoed in Zippy's ears.

Finally, the gentleman looked up from his whittling craft and said, "I am who you seek, but make it quick. I am tired of speaking with delinquents on the matter."

Zippy tapped his feet in anticipation. So, this was Clinsel, the retired knight. He looked very retired indeed with his unkempt beard and wrinkled clothing. "I assume you are the valiant Clinsel, retired knight?" Zippy inquired.

"Very astute," Clinsel muttered.

"We will take very little of your time. We know your ancestors were a part of the past dragon crusade, and you hold valuable information on the matter. Any details you care to spare on the matter?" Razil asked. She was straight to the point, and by Clinsel's amused smile, Zippy realized that was the right approach.

"Cutting to the chase. I can appreciate that in people. But what's in it for me if I give over such information? I've already turned down other adventurers on the same quest. What makes you different?" Clinsel asked, fixing his eyes back on his wooden craft.

"If I defeat the dragon, I will ensure there is a free homestead in your name on my land. Such information is valuable and will be paid in full with property," Razil replied bluntly but without curtness in her tone.

Clinsel looked at Razil with intensity, as if searching her very character with his eyes. Something earnest took over his previously annoyed expression. "How can I assure you will keep your word?"

"All I have is my word," Razil said as she removed the black glove from her hand and extended her palm in Clinsel's direction.

To Zippy's surprise, Clinsel shook Razil's hand. "Something about you I like. Well, like better than the other scum who have visited me, and you have offered me more than they." Clinsel looked side to side and said, "The red dragon has a lair in the middle of Blade Mountain, but only a fool would venture there without a dragon blade."

"A dragon blade? I thought those weapons were gone?" Dracklin asked with skepticism.

"That is not the whole truth. Most dragon blades have been lost or handed down for generations, and their significance has been lost by lack of knowledge," Clinsel replied.

"Where would we find such a blade? The dragon mentioned it being within the city walls, but I thought there was no way for that to be true," Razil questioned as she raked a hand through her short blonde hair.

"The forest witch that resides near Lake Bladesin would be the best place to start. She is not friendly to strangers but is the last to have seen a dragon blade. It is rumored that her ancestors helped craft them with the magic to penetrate a dragon's scale."

Heavy footsteps thumped behind them, the sound getting louder. By the chinking of metal, Zippy guessed it was a knight dressed in armor. Zippy's palms began to sweat. Surely, they had not done anything to be removed from the city already.

"Cousin! General Mattan spoke of your presence in the city. Is it true you seek to avenge Gar Thanik in the pursuit of the red dragon?"

Razil's blue eyes narrowed and turned to ice. Dracklin looked puzzled along with Clinsel, who scratched his grizzly beard as the man approached them. Zippy turned on his heel to face the nearing stranger.

The face that approached was that of a painting. He looked like a chiseled statue dressed in armor with a perfectly symmetrical face and droopy green eyes. His brown beard was elegantly trimmed to frame his thin lips, and his hair was shaved on the sides with a flawlessly coiffed top.

Seemingly oblivious to the icy reception, the man wrapped Razil in a tight hug. It was then that Zippy noticed the resemblance between them. It clicked. He must have been her cousin who had left Gar Thanik to pursue knighthood years prior. Razil's aunt and uncle spoke of him endlessly when Zippy joined in on family dinners. Razil rolled her eyes and patted his back as he released her.

"Hello, Blayne," she sneered.

Clinsel looked between them, then stood to his feet. "I will leave you to your family reunion. Remember, the forest witch is the only one who knows the secrets of our ancestors' past and how we were able to penetrate the dragon's scales. Go to her first, or you shall face peril."

"Does she have a name?" Razil inquired.

"That I do not know, but you will not mistake her," Clinsel answered as he left them and went inside the tavern.

Razil rubbed her forehead as she faced her cousin once more. "Blayne, that conversation was important."

The handsome man's expression turned solemn. "I did not mean to ruin anything. I was just happy to see you. It has been years."

Zippy extended his hand as he looked up at the golden boy. Blayne shook it back and looked Zippy square in the eye.

"I am Zippy. Razil's travel companion. It is wonderful to meet another link of Razil's family tree."

"Great. This is going to be a long day," Razil responded gruffly as she turned and walked into the tavern.

"Care to join us?" Zippy asked as he smiled at Blayne. He knew Razil would not be thrilled, but the man seemed kind, and it was clear he cared for Razil. Maybe some time in the tavern could relieve the tension.

"I am currently on duty. But I would love to later today."

"Excellent," Dracklin interrupted hastily. Zippy could not hide his puzzled expression as he looked at Dracklin. He did not usually take well to strangers.

Zippy grabbed at Dracklin's burly hand. "Come now, barbarian friend. We cannot let Razil drink without us."

Chapter 9

Let Her Die

They had been at The Tilted Tavern for what must have been hours. Razil lost count five beers ago and was enjoying the more nonsensical side of Zippy's riddles as his alcohol consumption increased. Luckily, the beer had not cost any of their coins after a couple of songs from Zippy's lute.

He was a sly fiend with those little strumming hands. If it weren't for her amulet, she would probably have already given him her day's wage. Dracklin already had until after each song, he would take his money back and scowl at Zippy. She and Dracklin always kept his magic a secret, knowing he would not fare well if others found out why they were so loose with their coin purses in his presence.

"I am so glad you let me join you on this little quest of yours. To defeat a dragon. It's a knight's greatest dream. Though I know the king forbade knights from joining this quest. For once, I need to break the rules for the good of Gar even if that means losing my knighthood," Blayne said with a gleam of wonder running through his eyes. He was no longer in his armor, and his hammer hung loosely at his hip.

"Who said you were joining us?" Razil asked.

"I thought another sword couldn't hurt anything," Drack said, followed by a burp.

"And when was this discussed?" Razil asked, beer churning aggressively in her stomach, anger bubbling in her veins.

"Well, when he and I went to grab the third round of beers, I said, 'You don't look like a complete ass. Are you any good with a sword?' And he said, 'Yeah', so naturally I invited him to join."

"Have you been possessed? Since when does Dracklin Mortim trust anyone? Especially someone in knight's armor. Or have you forgotten who brought you in chains to Gar Thanik in the first place?" Razil asked.

Drack blew out a frustrated breath. "Then let's vote on the matter. Who is in favor of Blayne joining us in our quest to vanquish the red dragon from our lands?"

Both Zippy and Drack responded in favor immediately.

"Zippy! Surely you jest," Razil said as she slapped an open palm to her forehead.

"What? I kind of like him. He reminds me of my cat, Pumpkin," Zippy replied, his eyes cheery.

"It's not even your cat, Zippy. It's Wes' to keep away the tavern rats."

Zippy just shrugged and started another riddle. In her annoyance, Razil tuned him out. Of course, Blayne would ruin this for her. He had always been the best to come from her family, and her friends would probably prefer him over her.

The tavern door creaked open, putting a sudden stop to Razil's self-pity. A very beautiful woman entered and stood in the doorway in a deep maroon tunic tucked into black breeches. She pushed back the hood from her black cloak. It was Alyssandra Landcaster—Lyss. Her hair framed her long, oval face perfectly, and her eyes narrowed at the sight of her staring. Razil looked away, and Lyss sauntered up the stairs as if Razil was not even there.

"Is that the Landcaster lunatic?" Drack asked with disgust coating his voice.

"I kind of like her, too," Zippy chimed in.

Drack looked down at their very jovial friend with a raised brow. "You like everyone."

"That is simply not true. I find some people boorish and others quite dull. But her, I like. She's feisty and cunning. Two things I can admire in a person," Zippy said as he took another gulp of his beer. The foam coated his red beard, causing him to sneeze.

"What do you think of that one, Razil? Surely you're on my side here. She did kidnap you," Drack insisted.

Razil's heart hammered as she thought of the beautiful woman, but instead she shrugged. "I did steal from her."

"Oh, by the wolf. Are you attracted to the Landcaster vampire? The very rich who exude their privilege, while you stole as a child to feed your mother? While I killed in a gladiator arena to entertain their bloodlust?" Drack shook his head and let out a disappointed snort.

"Who said anything about attraction?" Razil deflected. She knew where Lyss came from, but something about her seemed different.

"Razil, attraction is the only explanation for why you don't seem to mind the woman who had you tied up in her basement," Drack countered.

Razil scanned the table, looking for some support. Zippy chuckled, enjoying the banter. Blayne looked mortified and stared fixedly at the table. She chose not to respond and went to get another beer. When she returned to the table, the conversation had shifted, much to Razil's relief.

Razil lifted the mug to her mouth and froze. The foam rested on her lips, light and fluffy, as her eyes widened at the sight of him. He blended into the night, standing outside the window across the room, all black and no sound. She caught the flash of his haunting grey eyes from under his cloak's hood as he peered into the tavern.

Wolf.

She would know those eyes anywhere. He was up and gone in the split second it took to recognize him. A nauseating sensation swirled in Razil's stomach. Lyss was upstairs, readying herself for bed. Though she knew Lyss could hold her own, Wolf rarely lost and never left those alive to whom he felt revenge was owed.

He was not leaving that room with Lyss alive, knowing she was the leader of The Horned Lamb. And with Alyssandra Landcaster, the daughter of Gar Thanik's beloved councilor, outside of the city walls, she was much easier to kill without the watchful eyes of her guards. No one would be able to prove that Wolf had committed the crime.

Razil knew she should not care. If he killed her, one more obstacle keeping her from inheriting her own city in the Gar countryside was gone. Still, her mind raced. Razil knew her fondness for Alyssandra Landcaster, the rich and rude daughter of a councilor, ran deeper than she liked to admit. Razil had seen glimpses of her other side when Zippy entranced her peeking through all the anger in her eyes. Lyss, the brave, sweet, deeply passionate, and intelligent woman, faced this dragon's quest alone.

She shook the thoughts from her head. No, she was just attracted to her like Drack had said. That was all this was, but whatever the case, she was not about to let a beautiful woman die.

Razil dropped her mug on the table abruptly and jumped to her feet. "Wolf is scaling the wall outside and heading upstairs."

"If he wanted trouble with us, he would have confronted us. Surely, we have time for another beer before heading on our quest, though I know you wish to beat him to the information on the red dragon," Drack said as he slurped his beer.

"I think he means to kill Lyss," Razil said hurriedly.

"Lyss as in Alyssandra Landcaster? Though I don't mind her, I thought she was your competition and we were trying to steer clear of Wolf?" Zippy inquired with a confused look brewing in his hazel eyes.

"Yes, I understand how it sounds, but I'm going to save her. Meet me outside. If Wolf and his rogues are here, we must make haste to the forest witch before he gets there. It is only a matter of time before he finds our informant, and I am sure this city is reeking of his thugs by now."

"Leave the wretched girl and let us leave now, then," Drack rumbled.

"Meet me outside the city by the canal. I can handle Wolf alone," Razil said before racing up the stairs.

The three men muttered something, but they did not argue. Razil made quick work of the stairs, careful not to make a sound as she climbed. The adrenaline coursed through her veins and pounded in her ears as she strained to hear anything unusual.

A crash sounded from three doors down, and she ran towards it. She wanted the element of surprise, so she quickly pulled her lock-picking tools from her satchel. Heart racing, she worked on the lock nimbly, wincing as a body slammed into a wall and strangled cries echoed from the room. She moved her fingers quicker, trying to keep her breathing and mind calm until she finally heard a click.

She opened the door quietly to reveal Wolf pinning Lyss to the wall with his hands around her neck. Her dagger was on the ground next to her, and several of Wolf's daggers were stuck in the walls around the room, which was in complete disarray.

Lyss' dark eyes widened when she saw Razil, but she did not give away her position. Razil snuck behind Wolf with her saber drawn. As she swung at Wolf, he let go of Lyss' neck and avoided the blade's fall at the last second, turning to face her.

He picked up Lyss' jewel-encrusted dagger and lunged, the veins in his bald head bulging. "You fool, Razil!"

Wolf stabbed at Razil, but she parried easily. He swung like a madman, fury in his eyes, sweat covering his entire body. He was fatigued, and it showed in the lack of intensity in his blows. Razil could wait him out, block until he was completely exhausted, and slit his throat at his first mistake. But she knew Deelaz or one of his other rogues would arrive soon if they did not hear back from Wolf. His pack is what made Wolf the most powerful man in Gar Thanik. Their arrival would complicate her escape and hinder her getting to the witch before Wolf received intel. No. That would not do. Stealth and a quick escape were necessary.

Razil saw Lyss out of the corner of her eye, bent over, her chest heaving as she clutched at her neck. Then she saw her stand. Her dark eyes looked like molten metal, hissing and emitting heat from the forge. Lyss ran at Wolf's back, tackling him from behind. The dagger dropped from Wolf's hand.

Before he could grab it, Razil stomped his head with her boot and grabbed Lyss' arm. The barkeep appeared in the doorway with two knights. The commotion must have alerted them.

"What is all this?" he shouted.

Razil grabbed Lyss' hand. "Come on. We must go now!"

Though her eyes were skeptical, Lyss grabbed her dagger and nodded. Wolf staggered to his feet as Razil pulled Lyss along to make their escape. Razil wrapped her arms around Lyss' body and jumped out the window, throwing the grappling hook on her belt as she did, praying she did not miss.

Her heart thudded faster as they fell. Time seemed immovable as she felt the wind tousle through her hair. Lyss held her tight, burying her face in Razil's neck.

Clank.

Razil's heart lurched back into beating as they jerked to a stop. She hissed at the pain from the sudden halt. Regaining her senses, she quickly climbed the rest of the way down, grabbing Lyss' hand as soon as they hit the cobbled ground. She did not even bother to grab her grappling hook as she and Lyss ran as fast as their feet could until they reached the city's wall.

Their escape needed to be discreet. Wolf's rogues could be any-where. She checked the wall for a visible hole while staying out of the line of sight of the guards positioned on the walls and watch towers. Razil hoped Drack had enough sense to understand her preferred escape plan with the little instruction she gave him.

Finally, she saw it. An unnoticeable hole was hidden in a dimly lit section of the wooden wall. She looked at Lyss before scurrying over. "I know you do not trust me. But we both want two things. A name for ourselves, and Wolf dead. I think we will accomplish that more easily together than apart. Killing a red dragon will not be simple, especially with Wolf and his forces as our competition."

Lyss did not speak but nodded in agreement. She still had a red handprint around her neck, and her eyes were glassy. She smelled of fear and desperation, and Razil hated seeing her like that.

"In that case, follow my lead," Razil whispered as she crawled through the hole.

She helped pull Lyss through when she reached the other side. Crouching, she examined the wall, looking for guards who may have been alerted from their scuffle with Wolf, before running towards the canal leading to Lake Bladesin. Lyss followed close at her heel, silent on her feet.

When she reached the canal, the very wet heads of Drack, Zippy, and Blayne appeared. Blayne and Drack stood in the waist-deep water to reveal their torsos. Zippy must have stood the whole time because he was barely a chin above water as the others stood.

"Is she with us now, then?" Drack asked with a raised brow.

"I am," Lyss said calmly, her eyes emotionless. Razil caught Zippy empathetically looking at the red marking on her neck as she spoke.

"Hop in. The water is refreshing, and we'll leave fewer tracks this way," Zippy said as he wrung the water from his fabric cap and placed it back on his head.

"I sure hope private tutors teach rich girls how to swim in Gar Hocklin," Drack sneered.

Lyss ignored his comment and entered the canal. Razil glared icily at Drack, only to receive a shoulder shrug and an eye roll in return. She knew Drack was protective of her and had issues with Gar Thanik's old money. He would still be in Raufstig if not for the elite's urge to enslave barbarians and orcs to use for their gambling and amusement at the coliseum. Still, Lyss was useful, and if she trusted her, that should be enough for Drack.

Razil followed Lyss into the cool water. She felt the sweat and dirt on her skin washing away as they swam toward the canal's source: Lake Bladesin. They swam in silence, careful not to splash and ripple the water. Razi's clothing weighed her down, along with her weapons and thief's tools, but she swam nonetheless.

Hours later, they reached Lake Bladesin without being spotted by a knight of Gar Bladesin or one of Wolf's rogues. Razil exited the water, dripping, her clothes clinging to her body. She was exhausted, her legs shaking as she staggered away from the water. Zippy huffed and puffed as he shook out his favorite cap. Blayne looked chipper as ever, like a wet puppy, and Drack eyed him while trying to mask his exhaustion in a faux stretch of his arms above his head.

Razil looked at Lyss, whose clothes clung to her curves, her necklace glimmering in the starlight. Razil casually moved her gaze to Lyss' eyes only to realize where they roamed. Her eyes skimmed Razil's body, hovering hungrily as the wet fabric plastered itself to Razil's skin. When she caught Razil's eyes, Lyss quickly turned her head and pretended to be examining their surroundings. Razil had half a mind to call Lyss out for looking at her body, but chose to leave her be. Satisfaction warmed her chest as she realized her body had the power to make Lyss blush.

"Do you think we are a safe distance to make a fire?" Zippy inquired with hopeful eyes.

"I think it's best we descend into the trees on the west side of the lake before making camp," Blayne said as he pointed toward the dense woods surrounding Lake Bladesin. "Give us a little protection from the watchful eye of Gar Bladesin's knights in the guard towers. Or one of Wolf's rogues."

"I agree." The words left an odd taste in Razil's mouth. She often did her best never to agree with her cousin.

They trudged on until they reached the safety of the trees. Drack had a fire going quickly, and Zippy removed soggy cheese and assorted nuts he'd taken from the tavern from his satchel. It was disgusting but Razil devoured them, her stomach aching with hunger. After she hoofed down her food, she removed her tunic, breeches, and socks and laid them by the fire to dry. Zippy and Blayne followed suit. Lyss did not speak, but Razil felt her eyes once again on her body.

"Wet clothes are difficult to sleep in," Razil explained.

This time, Lyss did nothing to hide her wandering eyes. Lyss looked at Razil boldly as she removed her own shirt and breeches and placed them by the fire. The swell of her full breasts under her undergarments and the curve of her hips were intoxicating. Razil's heart stuttered, and heat billowed throughout her body. The look in Lyss' eyes let Razil know she was aware she had Razil's attention and could easily pull her under her spell. The men did not even blink in Lyss' direction, but it took all of Razil's self-control to tear her eyes away and walk off. She needed space from the day's hubbub and the unwelcome emotions that overwhelmed her in Lyss' presence.

Razil found a stump and sat as she stared at the tree tops, listening to insects. She could hear the laughter of the men around the campfire as they told each other jokes. Razil drowned them out and began daydreaming of the days ahead. She could almost taste the freedom of being a ruler of her own land.

She would have a cabin, and her closest friends would live nearby. Everyone would have space to settle and grow their gardens with access to clean water. Gar Razil would be a home to all who wanted a simple and quiet life. No gladiator matches or the rich squandering wealth on frivolities while the poor starved. No, Gar Razil would be different, a haven for all who worked hard and wanted an honest living.

Twigs snapped, startling her, and she jumped to her feet.

"It's just me," breathed Lyss as she emerged from behind a tree. Her clothes looked damp but much less wet than before as she stood with her maroon shirt tucked back into her black breeches. She had forgone the cloak, and her long hair was down and cascaded along her shoulders in black waves.

Razil gulped and sat back down on her stump. Lyss sat next to her, not picking up on the cue Razil was trying to send her that she had come into the woods for some alone time away from her. Lyss made her feel uncomfortable, and she only wanted to focus on her future.

Involving Lyss in the quest was a mistake made by her attraction. Drack was right; Razil should have let her die. Involving her could complicate the plan and wreak havoc on her ideas for Gar Razil if she successfully defeated the dragon. If Razil allowed Lyss' help in defeating Crimshyrbane, would there even be a Gar Razil? Razil shuddered.

Lyss looked at the goose flesh that formed on Razil's arms. "I am sure you are cold out here by yourself. Nights in spring can get chilly even though we're close to the Southlands. I brought you your clothes and satchel. They're mostly dry now."

Razil looked at Lyss' hands to see her holding her belongings. "Thank you."

"You're welcome. Zippy told me you need space to decompress after a day like today so I will leave you to it." Lyss stood and began walking back towards the laughing men, audible in the distance.

Razil smiled at Zippy's words. Her friend truly knew her. As Lyss turned, Razil realized she did not want her to leave. "Wait—stay. I mean, if you want to. You may stay if you want to. I know the boys' jokes are a lot. Also, Blayne and his golden boy facade is painful at best."

Lyss smiled a smile that reached her eyes. The small gap in her front teeth was visible, and Razil's cheeks flushed. She needed to get a hold of herself.

"It seems like you want me to stay. I also would not mind staying for a spell. I don't find Blayne insufferable, though," Lyss said as she sat next to Razil. Razil gagged at her last sentence, causing Lyss to giggle. "You're hard on him."

"You did not grow up with him. While I was stealing to live, he flourished, the only success to come from our family."

"Hmm. I am sorry your life held such pain at a young age," Lyss said with sincerity as she went to touch Razil's hand in comfort before retracting it slowly. She fidgeted with her fingers, awaiting Razil's response.

Razil felt skepticism rush to her head. She did not understand why Alyssandra Landcaster, the woman who hated every fiber of her being, was being nice to her. "I do not want your pity. My mother made her choices after my father passed, and I made mine. I do not regret my time with The Wolf's Teeth. It was a necessary evil, but now that is behind me and I am fine." She knew that saying she didn't have regrets was a lie, but she hoped Lyss would believe it.

"I do not pity you. You are not a stray kitten lost from its mother. But when I started The Horned Lamb, I saw Gar Thanik differently. I got a glimpse that was not clouded by my privilege or shielded by the gilded cage of my youth. I am sorry our society failed you, and the part my ignorance and privilege played in it."

Razil cast a look at Lyss that was dangerously infatuated. No one she had ever been attracted to had ever made her feel seen. Razil's eyes drifted to Lyss' lips, then down her neck. The red mark from earlier was bruising. Razil cursed Wolf's name in her mind as she reached out towards Lyss' neck. Lyss recoiled.

"I'm sorry. I just. Umm. I think I have something that may help. My aunt makes a salve that helps with bruising and cuts. Would you like some?"

Lyss nodded and ran a shaky hand through her hair. "Yes, that would be nice. But I have to be transparent about why I came here before you do."

Razil raised her eyebrow. "I was wondering why you left the warmth of the fire to sit by a woman with the charm of an ogre's breath."

Lyss laughed and pushed Razil's arm. "You were unbearable that day! And I thought you were one of Wolf's and targeting my family again," her voice turned somber, her eyes flickering with emotion.

The vulnerability of Lyss' words surprised Razil. She had seen glimpses of it under Zippy's music, but not of her own accord. Trust must have been gained after saving her life. She didn't want to press too hard and cause Lyss to retract, but she was curious.

"Again?"

Lyss paused, sadness taking over her features. "Wolf is responsible for my father's death."

Her words hit Razil in the chest in a way that hollowed it and sank to her stomach. For the first time, Lyss and The Horned Lamb made sense. This was all about revenge for her. Razil did not push Lyss to explain further but placed a gentle hand on hers and said, "I am truly sorry for your loss. Wolf is the worst kind of scoundrel."

"No need for apologies. My father's death is not on your hands." Lyss paused to wipe a stray tear from her eye. "I am here because I need to know something."

"What?" Razil asked, curious.

"Why save me? Why not let me die? I stand in the way of you obtaining the land from the king's decree. Even if we work together and defeat the dragon, I am sure you know I'll want a piece of the property and lead it. I do not wish to become councilor of Gar Thanik one day, though it would seem fit to most voters when my mother no longer wishes to run. Although my mother has advocated for and made some positive changes in Gar Thanik, corruption will always exist there. The king cannot upset the rich too much, or there would be an uprising. She knows I do not wish to lead on those terms, only making marginal differences to the most vulnerable while the wealthy keep their profits. Explaining to my mother that I wanted to establish my own city in Gar from the ground up was the only way she let me leave," Lyss said as she stared at Razil. Councilors must be elected in Gar Thanik, but Lyss was right, the people would choose her at her mother's retirement, and she would constantly be in her shadow, unable to enact any real change. Razil understood the desire to have something of her own.

Lyss looked at Razil, clearly annoyed by her silence. "Well, go on. I'm waiting."

Something about Lyss' general intensity and unabashed speech intrigued Razil, but this brought up a topic that Razil was not ready to be honest about, even with herself. She never wanted to let herself develop feelings beyond attraction for a woman, but something about Lyss lit a fire in Razil's heart she did not realize needed kindling. Her energy was heady, and Razil could not get enough of it. This feeling was all-consuming, but she did not fully understand what it was, just that she did not mind it.

"I have a feeling," Razil responded as vaguely as she could manage.

"And this feeling is?" Lyss questioned, not letting Razil worm her way out.

"That you are fated to be on this journey as I am. I cannot explain it to you further, but I think we are meant to be in this fight together," Razil lied.

"I find that odd. But you are odd in general, so maybe it makes sense," Lyss said with a smile crinkling her eyes. Razil turned away at the joke of her oddness. She had never felt like she fit in, especially with someone of Lyss' status. She was a thief and the daughter of a drunk mother and dead father, while Lyss was a highly educated daughter of one of the most powerful voices in Gar. One of only three that the king truly took into consideration.

Lyss grabbed Razil's shoulder and pulled her to face her again. "Please let me have some of your aunt's salve. I do not want the print of that monster to mark me in the morning."

Razil looked at her, contemplating her next move, then resigned to help her. Razil removed the salve from her satchel. The minty aroma tickled her nose as she gingerly applied it to Lyss' neck. Lyss winced.

"I'm sorry. I am trying to be soft." Razil whispered.

"It's not you. It's just tender. Please continue. I can feel it helping."

Razil took a deep breath and continued. She tried to keep her fingers featherlight so as not to irritate the skin further. Lyss' pupils widened, slowly leaning in closer, close enough that Razil could smell the sweetness of her breath and see the blush on her cheeks. Their lips were nearly brushing as she continued rubbing the salve into her neck, a gentle moan escaping Lyss' lips that made Razil swallow. Razil sucked in a breath at the realization. Lyss must also be attracted to her to have such a visceral reaction to her touch. How had they gone from hating to whatever this was in such a short span? Razil's head was spinning.

"You two are going to catch your death out here. We'll be putting out the fire soon. Might want to warm up before bed," Blayne said as he emerged from the trees. He clamored forward with his hammer hanging from the belt on his hip and his dwarven-made shield strapped to his back. He leaned his shoulder against a tree and stretched his wrinkled tunic with his hands as he looked at them, confused. He looked more like Razil remembered him from his youth without all of his knight's armor on and the dumbfounded look in his eye.

Of course, Blayne would be the one to interrupt this moment. He was always clueless about when his company was not wanted. Lyss jerked back and stood quickly before grabbing Razil's hand to help her up. Razil stomped haughtily towards the campfire without even a look in her cousin's direction. She hoped he did not see what she thought was about to be a kiss. Blayne could never keep his mouth shut, and she knew Drack would not like that.

She snuck a glance at Lyss as she reached the fire and was met with a knowing smirk. Razil sat next to Zippy, who patted her hand and smiled. She couldn't quite put a finger on it, but something in her heart felt lighter as she sat next to Zippy and looked across at Lyss.

CHAPTER 10

A TROLL OF A TIME

T he day was warmer than usual as sunlight flickered through the broad-leafed trees. Razil realized they were moving south, and that had a part to play in the weather. They had been wandering for two days, the forest getting denser with every step. Gar Bladesin was far behind them, and Razil kept her saber in hand, whacking at the thick brush as she moved.

Occasionally, Razil would catch Lyss out of the corner of her eye watching her with crinkled eyes and the occasional giggle as Razil struggled to make a path through the dense greenery. Something had shifted between the two of them. Razil did not know where it would lead, but she did know that she was growing fonder by the day of the woman with dark eyes and a fiery soul.

"I recognize that tree," Drack said as he pointed to a rather large tree with a twisted knot. A woodpecker pounded at its bark, as if mocking him.

"Drack, there are a lot of trees. Are you sure?" Razil questioned.

"I know that tree. We have been here before," Drack insisted, raking his hands erratically through his long hair.

"Are we lost? I get the feeling we are. Maybe I could look at Zippy's map..." Blayne said with a dumbfounded look on his face.

"Seriously, Blayne. Can you not question the obvious right now? Everyone is already exhausted and frustrated," Razil said, trying to keep her tone even but failing.

"I think he's just trying to understand the situation," Lyss interjected sympathetically in response to Blayne's pouting.

"Seriously?" Razil asked as she began hacking more furiously as she charged forward.

"Wait, Razil. Should we not stop and gather our bearings?" Zippy pleaded.

Razil ignored him as she rushed forward. She could feel twigs biting at her ankles as she stomped, and insects buzzed in her ears. Lyss standing up for Blayne irritated her more than she cared to admit. Everyone always took his side and treated him like a little prince. Something about him had always been likable, while something about Razil always made people want to look down their noses.

Razil lost track of time, and she could feel the sweat building on her neck as it dripped down her back. A gentle tug on her sleeved arm caused her to turn. The eyes looking back at her were dark and warm like honey fresh from the comb.

"Razil, why are you acting like this? Zippy can barely keep up. We are walking in circles, and you aren't listening to anyone," Lyss said in a pleading tone.

Razil studied her face; she softened but still had a sting in her chest. "Why don't you go talk to Blayne?"

Lyss crossed her arms and clamped her mouth together tightly as she looked Razil up and down. "So that's what this is."

"What?" Razil questioned, averting her gaze to the ground. Embarrassment began ringing in her ears as Lyss tore her apart limb by limb with her gentle yet stern gaze.

"Jealousy," Lyss stated simply, waiting for Razil to contest it.

Razil shot Lyss a heated gaze that all but screamed the emotion. She tried to keep her feelings at bay but failed miserably. All of this intensity in her heart and mind was new to her. She had never felt this way, and certainly not so quickly, especially since she was not even fully sure of what she was feeling.

Finally, Razil crossed her arms and asked, "Why would I be jealous of Doofus?"

At this point, the men had caught up, and Blayne placed a wounded hand to his chest at her words. Drack and Zippy kicked dirt and looked around awkwardly.

"I am too old for games, Razil. You are being immature. I know you feel what I have been feeling since you saved me. Be an adult and tell me how you're feeling, rather than stomping through the forest on a fool's quest."

Razil was lost for words and got stuck on three repetitions of, "I...Umm...."

"Great explanation," Lyss scoffed as she uncrossed her arms and walked over to Zippy, who was studying a rudimentary forest map.

"Wait, Ly—"

A knife whizzed past her left ear, nicking her skin. She gasped, jerking her head to the right to see where it came from. A woman in a black cloak stood there, arm extended. The woman's eyes were sinister as she smirked in Razil's direction.

"Deelaz Red, your aim is piss as always," Razil taunted.

Deelaz responded by pulling two throwing knives from under her cloak and releasing them in Razil's direction. One missed Razil by a hair's width while Razil parried the other away with her saber. Drack charged in her direction, expression set with determination. Blayne followed close behind with his hammer in hand.

Wolf emerged from the trees with five more rogues that Razil did not recognize from under their hoods. Two had crossbows pointed at Drack and Blayne's chests, who stopped in their tracks. Zippy raised his lute, but cried out as his hands were twisted behind his back, and he gurgled, struggling to breathe.

Razil saw one of the cloaked figures bearing a staff and whispering a spell in Zippy's direction.

Magic user.

Razil did not realize how strong Wolf's ranks had become. Fear crept down her spine. She did not know her enemy as well as she thought. He never had a wizard among his thieves' guild while she was there. Most humans possessing magic resided in Leedbriar and would find no reason to leave and join a thug like Wolf. So, he must have been a vile sort.

"Release him," Razil demanded stonily as she stared at Zippy's tortured frame.

"Bold of you to demand anything of me," Wolf sneered. He walked closer to Razil, clucking his tongue before continuing, "Give me the Landcaster rat, and I will be on my way."

"And if I don't?" Razil asked, fury rising through her chest. "Then I have two crossbows ready to fire bolts through your oafs' chests, and I don't know how much longer the ugly gnome can go without breathing," Wolf answered with an indifferent shrug.

Heat billowed up Razil's neck. Wolf knew the only way to hurt her was through her friends, and he was toying with her. He liked watching her squirm, knowing her only true vulnerability.

"If I go with you, will you leave them?" Alyssandra questioned from behind Zippy.

"You have my word," Wolf responded in a condescending tone.

"No," Razil said as she looked at Lyss. She was desperate. There was no way to win, but she could not bear Lyss sacrificing herself any more than losing her chosen family. She was paralyzed by the choice before her and stood stuck as if torn in half.

She did not have much time to contemplate it, though.

A rumbling in the forest halted everyone's conversation. The ground shook, and Razil lost her footing as the smell of rotting flesh filled her nostrils. The wizard holding Zippy broke the spell, and Zippy fell to his knees, gasping for air. Lyss wrapped him in her arms.

Everyone looked around in panic, trying to locate the source of the smell and the ground-shaking force. Before Razil could think, a large, ghastly figure ripped through the vegetation behind Wolf. All but one of his rogues jumped to the side, running into the trees. The one rogue who did not move quickly enough was snatched by the enormous hand of a forest troll. The rogue's head was quickly bitten off, and the creature chewed loudly on his skull.

Wolf and the rest of his rogues were nowhere to be seen. They fled, leaving Razil and her companions face-to-face with the monster that stood almost as tall as the trees.

"I don't think we can outrun this thing," Drack shouted while twisting Beatrice's shaft in his hands.

"Agreed," Razil confirmed as she swung her saber in front of her.

The forest troll roared as blood dripped from his putrid green lips. He beat his chest and bounded forward. Drack made it to the creature first, closely followed by Blayne. He attempted to swing his battle ax at the troll's leg, but had to tuck and roll at the last second to avoid the troll's fists. The ground shook violently, causing Blayne to trip, and he rolled to the side to evade the troll's wrath as he tried to regain his footing.

Razil rushed forward but had to jump to dodge the troll's swinging arms. Lyss crept from behind and seemed to go unnoticed by the beast as it swung wildly at Razil, Drack, and Blayne. If nothing else, Razil was happy to take the troll's attention off Lyss as she snuck to the creature's backside.

Lyss pulled the jewel-encrusted dagger from her hip, and Razil swore she saw the red gem on her necklace glow as she did. Lyss swiped at the troll's ankle tendon, drawing blood and an ear-piercing shriek from the monster. Razil celebrated a silent victory, but it was short-lived.

The troll quickly recovered, looking more angry than hurt. He turned quickly and grabbed Lyss in his massive hands before she could move away. Lyss' face turned beet red as the troll's grip tightened around her torso.

From the corner of her eye, Razil saw Zippy pull out his lute. A light, maternal melody soon rang through the clearing—the song of a lullaby. The troll stopped moving, and his eyes sagged as the song continued. Slowly, his hand loosened around Lyss, and she jumped free of his grasp.

Drack sprang forward with a lunging jump. As he landed, he swung his mighty ax through the troll's abdomen, exposing his intestines as he fell to the ground with a powerful thud.

Razil rushed to Lyss' side. "Are you okay?"

Drack rolled his eyes at her question.

"I'm fine, just some bruising in my ribs I think," Lyss responded.

"Can I see?" Razil asked.

Lyss rolled up her shirt to reveal swelling and darkening bruises around her rib cage. The sight was awful. Lyss saw the look in her eyes and abruptly pulled down her shirt before getting to her feet and looking around.

"I am fine," Lyss said, trying to sound as if she wasn't almost squeezed to a pulp. The toughness earned a nod of respect from Drack, but it deeply troubled Razil.

"Are you sure?" Blayne asked, his concerned features matching Razil's.

"We have a forest witch to find, and Wolf has a head start. My bruising will still be there in the morning. I can tend to it then," Lyss responded.

With that, the companions were on their way again, but Razil let the others lead this time.

CHAPTER 11

THE FOREST WITCH

Since the troll encounter, Razil had been far more bearable and willing to listen to reason. She fawned over Lyss like a lovestruck fool, and Zippy loved to watch the ice melt from her usually guarded eyes. Lyss tried to hide her pain, but was not as convincing as she thought. The troll had done a number on her, and he feared several of her ribs were broken. Her resolve was impressive, though, even Dracklin took notice and kept his previous negativity locked away as he resigned to find her a valiant warrior after all.

Blayne had taken over much of the navigation with Zippy's help. Gnomes were skilled with maps, and Blayne had significant training during his time as a squire at Gar Bladesin. Tracking and being able to navigate in uncharted areas was a part of their training to take up arms as knights.

Zippy was surprised by how well Razil had taken her cousin's lead through the forest, given her normally perturbed attitude toward him; however, her attention seemed so focused on Lyss that she had little room for much else. What an odd couple, Zippy thought, but he hoped that, though their meeting was hostile at best, some sort of love story could still come from them.

Zippy was a sucker for a good love story even though he experienced no romantic or sexual attraction himself. Still, he understood Razil had always wanted to be settled and in love, though she was loath to admit it. So, he could not help but silently cheer them on.

As he watched his friend grow emotionally, whether she knew it or not, something rustled in his chest. Since their journey began, that rustling had felt light and feathery, floating under his sternum like a dove spreading its wings in the sun. His journeys always started like this—light, fun, and freeing. But something lingered underneath this time like a dove that sat waiting. Under the wing of the dove was a snake ready to coil around the bird, trapping it there to wither and die under its stranglehold. The feeling started to squeeze into Zippy's chest.

He never imagined himself in one place, much to the dismay of his parents, who wished him to marry and have gnomish babies and remain in Berry Meadows forever. But he knew forever did not exist for him anywhere. His parents were kind and understanding. His father even let him spend time with the elf, Malachi the Orange, who lived amongst the gnomes, learning magic rather than helping him work at his family's little shop in the market. It was a nice life, but a life he just had to leave.

He spent time in Leedbriar furthering his bardic magic but found the people snobbish and self-absorbed. This led him to Kindrelve, where he met Thograyn Barhammer. Thograyn treated him like a son, letting him live rent-free in exchange for the gift of music. Eventually, the mines felt like a prison to Zippy, and he left Thograyn without even a note. Goodbyes had never been Zippy's strong suit. He was deeply compelled to leave, but the pain of hurting others still broke his heart. Though it left a hollow cave in him, the loneliness was never enough to keep him in one place or even have a proper goodbye.

He tried Gar Hocklin, and although the horses and the landscape were beautiful, it never sat quite right with him, which led him to his last spot, Gar Thanik. The bustling city was meant to be but a blip on the map of Zippy's adventures. A stop in his ill-planned grand scheme, but then something unexpected happened. He met Razil.

Her tortured eyes were calm but severe. She had lived through a heaviness most would not experience in their lifetimes, and regret radiated from her aura. She had a way of seeing past Zippy's lighthearted nature and into his very being. That grew a kinship between them like nothing he had ever experienced. Then, there was Dracklin, the emotionally complex brute of a man who would walk into death to spare a friend. They became a family like he had never known, growing bonds more profound than he'd ever expected to form.

But he knew himself. Their journey led to a certain permanence he did not think himself capable of. If he helped slay this dragon, they would inherit a piece of the Gar kingdom. Razil and Dracklin would expect him to be a founding member and set roots. Could he stay planted and settled in one area? Sometimes he thought of running into the trees, leaving his little search party behind never to find the dragon. At least it would save the disappointment of seeing his friends' faces when he said he wanted no stake in Gar Razil and would resign himself to adventure again without another word.

He knew logically his friends would be okay with him traveling and keeping in touch, but that was just it. Something always pushed him to leave and never look back. Would he do the same to those he had grown to love most? The thought made him shudder.

Blayne's chipper voice interrupted Zippy's silent panic, which was masked in a whimsical smile. "I think we found our mark," Blayne said, sounding like a sing-song bird on a summer day.

Zippy looked up to see what Blayne was pointing at. It was an old cottage with a straw roof. The siding had seen better days as vines crept up the outer walls and caressed the windows. The door looked busted open, creaking slightly with the breeze. Boot prints marked the path to the doorway, and Zippy feared they had been beaten to the forest witch by Wolf. He prayed to Zajac that she was still alive, but feared the worst.

Dracklin pulled his battleaxe from his back and looked over his shoulder. "Better be prepared upon entrance. It seems others have been here recently."

Razil nodded in agreement. "Wolf usually leaves without a trace. The door and boot marks are meant to send a message. He wants us to know he has us beat."

Alyssandra inhaled through her front teeth and blew a small whistle as she pulled the dagger from her hip. She pulled down the hood of her cloak, and a waterfall of dark hair danced around her shoulders.

"His messages do not scare me," Alyssandra said as she bounded towards the cottage.

The air felt charged as it entered Zippy's lungs. A second passed as he contemplated the sensation. Not charged. Magical.

"Wait, Alyss—" But he could not finish his sentence before Alyssandra was wrapped in a web, illusory spiders crawling around her skin and digging into her flesh. Wolf's wizard must have set a trap.

Alyssandra clawed at her skin as she screamed incoherent sobs. The magical creatures nipped at her skin, and the web tightened its grasp on her body.

Razil started to move towards her, panic stark in her features.

"No, Razil! This is a trap set by Wolf's wizard. There could be other webs," Zippy pleaded with her.

Razil looked at him and removed her saber from its sheath. "We cannot allow her to withstand this torture, Zippy! She will die."

A groaning sound came from the cabin, mixed with Alyssandra's screams and Razil's anxious huffing.

Good, Zippy thought. The witch may live if the groaning belonged to her. How much life was left was the question. The witch would surely have the ability to reverse this wizard's spell. He needed to find a way through this trap to get to the witch and save Lyss.

Zippy took in a deep breath and allowed himself to feel the magical aura. The spell was nasty and twisted. He could feel the darkness of the wizard who uttered it. It made his spine tingle in the same way it did when an insect scurried across the floor. He drowned out the outside noise and only allowed himself to feel the uncomfortable frequency of this dark wizard's soul, and then he felt a shift to the left of Alyssandra that led to the door. It was a tunnel of a different energy. Earthy. Serene, with the smell of mud and moss.

The forest witch. She must be alive from within and barreling through the other wizard's trap, calling to him.

"Zippy, I am going. We cannot wait any longer!" Razil yelled.

"I agree," Dracklin countered.

Zippy put up his palm and opened his eyes. "No. I will go. I can sense the spell, and I think I have found a hole that leads to the forest witch. If I am correct, she will be able to reverse this spell. She is calling to me now."

"Kill me! I can't take this," Alyssandra bawled as she tore at her skin.

"It is unlikely Wolf left the witch alive, Zippy. Lyss needs us now," Razil argued as she moved closer to Alyssandra.

"Stop!" Zippy yelled as loud as his lungs could bear. Dracklin and Razil stared at him, stunned by his outburst. "I know you think I am just a swindler who plays his lute for coin. A funny friend with a riddle and not a care, but I am made of more, and she is calling to me. I can feel the forest witch paving the way for me through this trap. I am the only one suited to do this, and I need you to trust me."

Razil and Dracklin stood silently for a moment before anyone spoke.

Blayne touched Zippy's shoulder and said, "We trust you."

With that, Razil and Dracklin nodded.

Zippy closed his eyes once more. Alyssandra's screams quieted, and he only let himself feel the strong pull of moss and mud lead his steps through the tangle of destruction surrounding him. The more steps he took, the stronger the witch's aura and the quieter the dark magic became.

"I am here, gnome. Get my healing potion off the ground over there where the thugs discarded my things," a raspy voice wheezed.

Zippy opened his eyes and realized he was in the cottage's doorway. The room in front of him was in complete disarray. Books were ripped from shelves and soaked in liquid from shattered potion bottles. The fabric furniture was torn and shredded, and a woman lay in the middle of the mess, clutching her chest over her patchwork dress of many muted tones of tan.

Her silver hair frizzed out and covered her eyes as she pointed toward the mess of potions and books on the floor. "Green potion with golden flecks," she whispered through labored breathing.

Zippy rushed to grab the potion she was pointing at and brought it to her lips. She drank the potion earnestly, and the life seemed to glow from under her features as her once-frail frame began to heal and she sat up. She stood without warning and rushed outside.

The woman yelled spells that Zippy did not understand, and soon the web surrounding Alyssandra dissipated as the spiders on her flesh burned away. Other webs previously hidden began to burn and lift away as the witch moved her hands, chanting consistently. When the spell was lifted entirely, Alyssandra dropped to the ground, Razil rushing to catch her as she fell. Dracklin and Blayne rushed to her side, surrounding her.

"Move," the witch directed as she shooed them away with her wrinkled, brown hands. She chanted further, and Alyssandra opened her eyes, breathing returning to normal. "Come, child, I healed the damage from the wizard's spell, but I sense another injury in your ribs that a potion can heal," said the witch.

Zippy saw Razil's eyebrow quirk, and she looked like she was about to protest, but then she sealed her lips and followed the witch into her cottage. Everyone else followed behind.

The witch moved her hands around erratically, chanting in a language Zippy did not understand. Books returned to shelves, potions to bottles, and the fabric furniture repaired its ripped stitches.

When she finished, she walked over, picked out a potion similar to the one Zippy had fetched her moments before, and brought it to Alyssandra. "Drink," the witch said, pushing her silver curls from her dark brown eyes.

Alyssandra looked at the swirling contents skeptically. "Who are you?"

"Well, I am Hanni, but you probably know me as the forest witch. Reclusive and the keeper of secrets. Now, drink. Unless you have been enjoying your broken ribs setting in a disjointed manner."

Alyssandra still looked skeptical, so Zippy chimed in, "She drank a similar brew herself if that calms your nerves."

Alyssandra glanced at him thankfully before swallowing the contents whole. The concoction caused her to cough and sputter as she grabbed onto the red-encrusted jewel that lived around her neck. Hanni's eyes darted to the jewel, widening slightly as she waited for Alyssandra to quit coughing to speak.

"Ahh. I haven't seen this friend in a while," Hanni said as she placed a delicate finger on the amulet that caused so much commotion when Razil stole it.

Alyssandra pulled away, clutching the amulet close to her chest. "You know it?"

"Yes, my husband made it during the dragon crusade before his passing. Do you bear its twin?" Hanni asked.

"Your husband lived during the dragon crusades? That was lifetimes ago. Over five hundred years," Razil countered in disbelief, arms crossed protectively over her chest as she took a defensive step toward Alyssandra.

"Calm now, child. Time is meaningless to someone of my power. My husband was not so fortunate in his gifts, but my love was an excellent creator of magical elements. His specialty was in weapons that could penetrate a dragon's scales. And that necklace pairs with an enchanted dagger named Dragon's Bane."

An indecipherable look flashed in Alyssandra's eyes, gone in a second. She fumbled at the sheath resting on her waist beneath her black cloak. "Is this the dagger you speak of?"

Hanni clapped her hands in excitement. "Dragon's Bane!" She stretched her hands out. "May I?"

Alyssandra hesitated but then put the blade's hilt in Hanni's trembling hand. "My Tarick. I can feel him in this blade. His magic is like a balm to my soul," Hanni said, her dark eyes glazed over as tears fought to escape. "And I see some of him in you. The eyes. Yes, the eyes."

"What do you mean?" Alyssandra questioned.

"My dear husband had a brother, who bore these weapons during the dragon crusade. He had a family and though we lost touch, it seems the weapon was passed down," Hanni explained.

"My father was the ancestor of its wielder, your husband's brother?" Alyssandra asked.

"It seems so dear," Hanni said with a sentimental gleam.

"How can you know for sure?" Razil asked as she raised an unconvinced brow.

"I just do. I can feel it," Hanni whispered more to herself than them. She inhaled a breath, looked at the crowd in her home, and started talking.

She told them of her husband and how he made weapons. Details irrelevant to their journey spouted from her mouth as well as instrumental facts about how the blade worked in conjunction with its amulet pair. She explained how the magic of these two artifacts worked together to pierce the seemingly impenetrable scales of the evil red dragons. Zippy and his friends listened without a word, letting her talk. It was obvious a friendly ear was not commonplace in her reclusive cottage. She ended her monologue with, "I am so glad that bastard was not the wielder of such a weapon. My love would have despised him. But you, dear girl, though prideful you are, I can sense good in you, and my dear Tarick would have loved it if the weapon stayed in the family."

"By bastard, do you mean Wolf?" Dracklin asked.

"Aw, yes. I believe that was his name. He came wanting answers about how to kill the red dragon, but I could sense the rot inside him. His intentions were not pure. I told him very little of a blade he would never wield and nothing more. I assumed it is why I am still alive. Just in case he can't find Dragon's Bane and needs to come back to attempt to gain more information from me."

"Are there no others like Dragon's Bane?" Blayne asked, green eyes shining.

"Perhaps in another time or place. They have since been given to the Elves of the south and lost in other regions far from here. Dragon's Bane is the last I can sense in Gar," Hanni responded.

She continued explaining more history and eventually Razil thanked her for her information as she bid her goodbye. Hanni hugged each of them as they left, her quirkiness appreciated by his friends. He could tell by their brightened eyes and soft smiles.

Zippy looked at Hanni once more and thanked her for her help. Hanni reached for Zippy's arm before he could follow his friends. Her feeble hands wrapped around his wrist like a vice, scalding him to the touch. "New friend, remember these words. You will have a choice to make. Leave, like always, or finally stay. Know that your friends' lives will be at stake," Hanni whispered so that only Zippy would hear.

"What does that mean?" Zippy pleaded. He leaned closer to Hanni, hoping she would elaborate.

Hanni shook her head and gave him a wink. "Ta ta." She whisked away into her cabin, whistling into the air without another word.

Chapter 12

Heartbeats

It had been several days of traveling since their visit with Hanni. The forest was thick, and they were making headway toward the Blade Mountains, growing closer with each passing day. Their pace had been hurried as they nipped at Wolf's heel, desperate to be the first to reach the powerful red dragon's lair. Wolf's power was tenfold now that he possessed a fierce wizard. Razil was afraid a wizard of that power might stand a chance against the dragon.

They had a key he did not possess, though. Dragon's Bane was carefully strapped to Lyss' person. Razil wondered how long it would take him to work out that Lyss was holding such a weapon.

She had a sinking sense in the pit of her stomach that he would figure it out, and just as they were following his trail, he would eventually be tailing them. With his psychotic wizard, she wondered if they could win that fight. If the troll had not interrupted their last encounter, death would surely have taken them.

Night came as quickly as day, and Zippy announced they should settle in for the evening. Drack made quick work of a fire, and Blayne emerged with two rabbits he had hunted from the forest for them to share. Zippy would not eat them, but he'd foraged some berries for himself earlier as they walked. Lyss smiled at Razil from over her shoulder, and the twinkle that reached her eyes was enough to make Razil's heart flutter.

The feeling was almost overwhelming, and she needed time to figure out what was causing these reactions from just a look from Lyss' endless eyes. She could not understand why her feelings had grown so strong, and if it was mutual or nothing but a fleeting attraction.

As Razil normally did, she stole away from the fire and into the night alone. She loved her friends but needed time to gather her strength for the journey ahead and process the beating wings in her stomach that flapped in a frenzy every time Lyss gave her attention. She was exhausted emotionally and socially and desperately needed solitude. She found a spot in the soft dewy grass among the trees, laid flat on her back, and stared up into the stars.

Her thoughts went blank as she watched the constellations, the insect sounds chirping in her ears. The melody soothed her as the creatures squeaked and scurried along the forest floor. The approaching sounds of soft footsteps did not startle her as they had in the past. She recognized the gentle tread and felt oddly comforted by it despite it belonging to the very person who had stirred her heart into such confusion.

"May I join you?" Lyss asked as she stood behind where Razil lay.

Razil patted the ground next to her. Lyss slipped next to Razil with her shoulder a hair's distance away. The warmth of her body radiated, causing Razil's heart rate to increase and then calm. Lyss did not speak, simply staring at the stars with Razil. It was... peaceful. Her presence did not hinder Razil's ability to replenish her wits like she thought it would.

The way Lyss could just be with her in silence was like nothing Razil had ever experienced. It wasn't an awkward silence or tense. It felt right, like two humans having a comfortable experience together that words didn't need to pierce. She lay there for a while, just basking in the silent comfort of the stars and Lyss' presence. When she felt fully rested, Razil peeled away from the stars to take in a more beautiful view.

The moonlight illuminated Lyss' oval face, and her raven black hair poured around her head, dampening in the grass. Her chest rose and fell like the tide, her breasts softly moving with every inhale and exhale. She was the most stunning person Razil had ever seen. Something about her aura drew Razil in, making her want to know every detail of her body and soul.

Lyss turned to meet Razil's stare. Her face flushed, and her pupils widened. "Why are you looking at me like that?"

Razil let out a breath. "I just want to know everything about you." Razil couldn't help but look at Lyss' full lips as she spoke.

Lyss rolled her eyes and blushed further. She leaned in closer to Razil. "Is that your way of saying you want to kiss me?"

Lyss' boldness took Razil off guard. "No... Well, yes. I do, but I am not just saying what I think you desire to hear. I truly want to know you. Who is Alyssandra Landcaster? What was her childhood like? Her family? Her dreams? What makes her angry, sad, and joyful? What fills her heart with gratitude?" Razil asked quickly as she tore her eyes from Lyss, embarrassed by her confession. Speaking so freely and vulnerably was like itching a scab she desperately needed to relieve, but was afraid would start to bleed again. Razil had had many physical lovers, but this emotional intimacy was something she never fathomed.

Lyss giggled, making Razil even more self-conscious as she stared into the night.

"I am surprised you called me by my actual name," Lyss said as her eyelids fluttered. She brushed her hand against Razil's cheek, and Razil could feel her skin heating beneath her touch. "No need to be embarrassed, Razil. I think you are sweet."

The past hostility between them seemed like it had never been. Things had changed on this journey, and Razil could not be happier, even though it scared her. Razil stared at the stars, trying to keep her fear of attachment at bay.

Lyss grabbed her head more firmly and turned Razil's face to look at her. "I am serious. I want to see your gorgeous blue eyes while I bare my soul to you and bore you to death in the process."

Razil blinked back the look of surprise that was surely evident in her eyes from having Lyss' hands on her face and tangled in her short hair. "Nothing about you is boring to me."

Alyssandra grinned and loosened her grip; her fingers now softly intertwined in her hair. Her lips slightly twitched upward as she said, "My childhood was fairly common for my status. Like you, I was born during the Orc Wars. My father was a knight. He was away most of my childhood, so my mother mostly raised my brother Thadrick and me by herself. She was kind and smart, and I did my best to learn from her even before she was voted councilor. At age eight, my mother sent us to Gar Hocklin to go to school. She wanted us to be further from Gar Thanik in case the orcs made it past our southern city and into Gar Thanik. See, I told you, very boring."

"I am hanging on every word," Razil said with a smirk.

Lyss stopped gently caressing Razil's cheek and shoved her shoulder instead. Razil laughed, then grabbed her hand as she said, "Please continue. It is nice to hear about a normal childhood where a mother isn't an alcoholic and children do not steal to eat."

Lyss rubbed a circle so gingerly in her palm that it made Razil's heart squirm at the comfort of it. Lyss looked sympathetically into Razil's eyes, but she didn't want her pity.

"I'm waiting," Razil said with a teasing lilt.

Lyss let out an exasperated breath and laughed, releasing Razil's hand. "Fine. Gar Hocklin was lovely. It was much smaller than Gar Thanik, and there were horses everywhere. I spent most afternoons riding with my brother, and it was a simple time. At fifteen, my mother was elected councilor of Gar Thanik, and I moved back home. I always wanted to lead and be in politics, so I mentored under her, learning everything I could. The more I learned, the more I realized the time it would take to right the wrongs of our ancestors and close the wage gap. So, I guess you can say that becoming a leader for the people who fought for an equitable future became my passion at that young age. The Orc Wars ended shortly after I began mentoring with my mother, and my father returned. My brother stayed in Gar Hocklin. He grew to love the countryside more than the bustle of the city and had little desire for a life of politics. We visited him often, and my life felt whole for a while." Lyss' eyes grew misty, and she turned to face the stars.

Razil squeezed her hand. "If you do not wish to speak more, I respect that. But, if you are afraid to speak because it will make you emotional in front of another person, know that I want to hear anything you want to say and I have space for you in my heart."

Lyss wiped her eyes, turned to face Razil once more, and said, "It was my twenty-fifth birthday, so my father left patrol early to come home and celebrate. He was still a knight at the time, you see, and didn't enjoy the fame that came with my mother's political status and stayed in the background, mostly busying himself with his work. That day, I waited in my room and looked out the window, watching for him. When my father was close to our home, I saw Wolf emerge from the shadows with two rogues dressed in all black. I couldn't make out who they were. They grabbed my father as Wolf interrogated him on the streets. I saw Wolf grab a necklace from his neck and drop it as if burned. I ran down the stairs trying to get to him in time to save his life, but by the time I reached him, my father was dead, killed for a couple of gold coins and a necklace. I still don't understand why no knights or guards were patrolling that street."

Tears streamed down Lyss' cheeks, and her skin was a blotchy red. She took a deep breath and continued, "Anyway, that's when I vowed to bring Wolf to his knees before eventually killing him. I started The Horned Lamb. Stealing from Wolf and giving it back to the impoverished he takes advantage of. He has a secret store of treasures that he has been harboring underground. Theona used to work for him, and we have been scheming to break in and take all the wealth he's hoarded from the people he claims to be saving. And now I am a thirty-two-year-old woman on a wild quest with a reckless woman to slay a dragon and start the type of community I have always dreamed of."

A pit settled in Razil's stomach as realization crept into her sternum and crawled up her throat, suffocating her. The image of Wolf burning his hand all those years ago flashed before her eyes. Her heartbeat increased as blood rushed to her head. Her protection amulet, with its small gold chain and black pendant, singed into her skin.

Lyss shook her head and looked up into the stars. She wiped her eyes and said, "I am sorry for all the tears. I should not have burdened you with my baggage."

Razil squeezed her hand tighter and breathed out words as her consciousness flitted between the present and her regretful past, "You are never a burden. I lo—" Razil cut herself short. How could she claim to love Lyss after the pain she had inadvertently caused her?

Lyss turned and tangled her fingers in Razil's hair. She moved so close that Razil could taste the sweetness of her breath.

"Please finish that sentence," Lyss whispered against Razil's lips.

Razil's body desperately wanted to scream the words and kiss Lyss until the sun came up, but the guilt rampaging in her heart would not allow it. "Lyss, I cannot."

Hurt flashed across Lyss' face as she whispered, "Why?"

There was no easy way to say what must be said. A boulder sat on Razil's chest as she beheld the confused and wounded look swirling in Lyss' eyes. Razil closed her eyes and sucked in a deep breath before blurting out, "Lyss, I killed your father."

There was surely a more tactful way to deliver this information, but Razil's mind was racing out of control. Emotions consumed her.

Lyss' eyes filled with tears, and she shook her head in disbelief. "You would never. Why are you saying this?"

Razil trembled and vomit burned her throat, but she swallowed it back down. She took a deep breath and confessed, "You know I worked for Wolf. I remember the night you speak of. The necklace burned Wolf because he was not the hand that killed its bearer. Your father had a protection amulet he obtained from an Orc Shaman during the Orc Wars. It was not a random attack for some jewelry or coin. Wolf had planned the heist but did not fully understand how the amulet worked. After I killed your father at Wolf's command, the necklace called to me as its new owner, rejecting Wolf, and I've worn it since. This necklace has kept me alive, but at what cost? I hate it, and I never speak of it. The shame is too much to bear."

Alyssandra scrambled to her feet and backed away from her. Anger boiled on her flesh, her skin red and shaking. She spat out, "Razil, stop talking."

"I am so sorry. I left after that night. I left Wolf. I did not want to kill your father. But those who defied Wolf's commands ended up at the bottom of Blue Lake along with their family members. I am so sorry," Razil said on a shaky breath.

"You are the worst kind of monster, Razil. A coward who blames their evil doings on circumstance." Alyssandra huffed out intense breaths as her eyes impaled Razil with unbridled rage.

"You are right. I have no excuse. I am so sorry. I hate who I was, but I am not that person anymore," Razil pleaded as she tried to grab Alyssandra's hand.

Alyssandra moved her hand and looked at Razil with disgust. "Do not touch or speak to me, Razil Morganth."

Razil pulled the amulet from around her neck. "Please take this. It belongs to you more than me."

Alyssandra touched the amulet with revulsion in her eyes. It burned her fingertips, and she pulled back her hand with a hiss. "Keep your vile amulet," Alyssandra said as she shook her hand in pain and stormed into the forest.

Razil did not run after her. Alyssandra had every right to hate her. Razil wondered if she should let Alyssandra lead the men in their group and go off alone—she knew Alyssandra would make a better leader. The skeletons of Razil's past haunted her, and there were too many to rule a land.

Her stomach gurgled, and her chest felt hollow. Even though she did not deserve it, she realized something as they spoke earlier. Razil loved Lyss. She did not understand how or why, but she loved her and wanted what was best for her. Alyssandra may have been vengeful and at times a hot head, but after what she had been through, it was justified. She still had goodness, life, and kindness in her, regardless of the loss she had endured.

The fierce yet soft Lyss had broken a shell that enveloped Razil's very being, and she knew it could not be mended. Razil decided she should gather her things and leave. She loved her enough to know Alyssandra did not deserve to be trapped on a quest with her father's murderer.

Reluctantly, Razil pushed herself off the ground and trudged towards the campfire. When she arrived, the men looked at her sullenly, and Alyssandra was nowhere in sight. Dread ensued in Razil's chest. Surely, she would not venture alone in the creature-infested forest.

"Where is Lyss?" Razil asked.

"Why don't you tell us?" Drack answered. He had grown to respect the woman he used to despise. Time with her would do that to a person. Razil knew firsthand.

Razil took a deep breath. "I told her the truth in the forest, and she stormed off. I've come to gather my things and leave so she can travel with you instead of me."

"She has unfortunately beat you to it. She gathered her things and left with no explanation. Only that she was glad to have made friends and that she needed to leave," Zippy chimed in with a tear forming in his usually jovial hazel eyes.

Blayne averted his eyes, and the shame it caused made Razil lightheaded. She was truly a monster. How could her friends possibly still love her when they knew some of the horrors she had committed when she worked with Wolf?

"I owe you all an explanation. I should have been the one to leave, not Lyss. I realized something earlier when she spoke of the night her father died." Razil cleared her throat. It felt raspy and like her body had been drained of all liquid. She pulled the protection amulet from under her shirt and threw it on the ground. "When I worked for Wolf, I killed a man over this necklace. It was meant for Wolf, but the amulet rejected him because I had killed its bearer, not him. The necklace called to me at the man's death, and that night has haunted me since. Turns out the night of my greatest regret is also the night of Alyssandra's greatest pain. The man was her father. I understand if you no longer look at me the same or wish to travel with me."

Razil felt bile rise in her throat as she said it. She could barely stomach standing in front of her friends as shame washed over her.

The men were silent but for Zippy, who was actively sobbing and blowing his nose with a handkerchief. Blayne looked lost, and Drack's eyes were dark and unreadable. It made Razil's skin itch. How could she stand here any longer?

Razil began to gather her satchel and adjusted the saber on her hip. She turned on her heel and began to walk into the forest. A strong hand clasped her shoulder, spinning her around. She turned to face Drack, who wrapped her in an embrace. Her face rested on his bare chest, and the hairs tickled her nose. The squeeze was so tight she felt the air leaving her lungs, but she felt safe. Without realizing it, tears streamed down her cheeks hot and wet. He said everything without saying a word and as he released her, she wiped her eyes.

"Razil, we all know the things you did in your past to survive, and we love you as our dearest friend. You are not your greatest regret or the evils forced on you by an evil man," Zippy said from behind Dracklin. He stepped to where Razil could see him, and his eyes shone with an empathy that made Razil's chest tighten.

"I do not deserve your love. Wolf may have been the instigator, but I fulfilled the action. I stole. I killed people," Razil said through trembling breaths.

"Razil, you know of my profession. I have killed many who were surely someone's family. And unlike you I did not quit when I was released from my bondage. I am in no place to judge what you have done. Did you enjoy your time with Wolf?" Drack asked.

"No. I hated it. I loathed every second. But part of me was angry. Angry at the wealth some people held while I was hungry and broken," Razil admitted.

"Your anger is just. We live in a country where people starve while others feast and play. You were only a girl when your father died, and your mother turned to the bottle and isolated you from our family. You did your best to survive in a twisted world that does not benefit people in your circumstance. And perhaps you have done unspeakable things, but you also survived. Many others have died in such environments. You have to forgive yourself, Razil. In your past, you acted out of fear, desperation, and necessity. But you are not that person anymore. You haven't been in over seven years now. Razil, I would not follow any other into a dragon's lair," Blayne said as he looked at her boldly with glassy green eyes.

Razil looked at her cousin and felt seen. He knew her. He knew her family and her pain. This was part of the reason she had found him so intolerable. He had seen her in her youth before she was her own woman. When she had holes in her clothes and no shoes, with an empty belly. He knew the despicable things she had done with Wolf, and yet he loved her. He cared for her like a brother.

Razil cried, not a gentle cry, but a sob that left snot on her cheeks and her body shaking. All three men embraced her, and for a moment, some of the pain that gripped Razil seemed to be alleviated.

CHAPTER 13

A BOG OF NIGHTMARES

The days after Alyssandra's departure had been solemn. Razil barely spoke or ate, and her eyes had a dull emptiness that worried Zippy. Dracklin and Blayne tried to keep everything moving and the mission on track, but Alyssandra's absence was palpable. Zippy had not realized how close he'd grown with her until she was gone. He hoped their paths would cross again so their friendship would be rekindled. Most of all, he hoped Razil would forgive herself and reconnect with what he suspected was finally growing into more than a friendship. She deserved love and happiness. He could only hope that Alyssandra could find it in her heart to forgive Razil.

They'd exited the forest several days prior. Zippy was glad not to be stumbling over tree roots anymore, even if the grass in some areas was now up to his chest, creating new problems for his short legs. The grassland was getting softer with every step as they trudged along. The humidity hung in Zippy's lungs like bad smoke, and his brow was constantly covered in a sheen of sweat. The breeze from the East was welcome, but Zippy also feared they had met their next obstacle: the bog.

Zippy had never entered the bog, but he had heard the stories. The bog was formed after a great battle between the dwarves and elves of old. Previously, both races inhabited the mountains of the north, but one betrayal led to another, and the nations warred against each other. The dwarves were pushed south as the elves inhabited the mountains, but the elven leader, Jekenith, heard rumors of the dwarves rallying to fight for the mountains once more.

Jekenith gathered his forces and met the dwarven army led by their king, Smashl, in the center of Varki. The battle lasted for days, until a mighty storm burst through. Lightning, thunder, and flooding rains lashed down on the battling beings. Smashl killed Jekenith with a hammer to the skull, and the Elvin forces crumbled after their leader's death. The dwarven forces slew every elf in that battle, and their bodies were trapped under the flooding waters.

The dwarves left the cursed land and charged north to reclaim Kindrelve, their home in the mountains. The elves were forced as far south as Varki allowed, where they established Synllshara. Still, the souls of the elves who fought in the battle with Smashl remained in what is now the bog.

They could have traveled through the forest back to Gar Bladesin and then made their way to Blade Mountain, but given their last encounter in the city, the group chose to forgo this path. Traveling too far south would put them in danger of a run in with a barbarian tribe. So, they decided to travel through the bog, and they had little time to lose. Chances are, Wolf had already made his way through these lands based on some of the tracks that resemble footprints in their current location. Zippy hobbled along, lute strapped to his back, and hoped for the best.

"We're here," Dracklin announced, making a grand, sweeping gesture with his arm.

Zippy looked into the horizon to see the wetlands with pockets of plant debris. The breeze intensified, and he could feel the dark magic swirling around him. "We need to be careful as we move through these lands. Spirit remnants from wars of the past still live here. Dark magic is holding them to this place. Do not step into the deep waters, or you may not step out."

Razil shuddered, and Blayne let out a noticeable gulp. Zippy's arms were covered with goose flesh, and his usual cheer was replaced by dread. Dracklin took the first steps forward, and the soft ground rose to his ankle.

Razil and Blayne followed behind, trudging carefully through the soft plant mass, the wind blowing their clothes and hair as they moved. Zippy reluctantly followed behind. His legs were much shorter, and the bog exhausted him as he moved through. He fought against the land with every step to keep from being sucked below.

The deeper they descended into the bog, the thicker the air became. The breeze stifled, and a misty fog covered their line of sight. He pushed his legs forward with all his might, the soft ground trying to engulf him. Whispers started creeping from the ground, but he paid them no mind until they were so loud he could no longer ignore them.

"Zippy Redbeard, running again. When will you stop this madness and return to the burrows where you belong? A jolly singing gnome with a family, that's what you need," his mother's voice bellowed.

"Time to settle down, Zippy. Start a family. You are the age for settling," his father chimed in.

"Stop it. I do not want to marry and have children. I need to feel free to wander; the burrows are not my home anymore," Zippy whispered.

"You bring shame to the Redbeard name. Your poor father left to work alone, brokenhearted. And I left with no one to taste test my pies," his mother said, shame infused in her voice.

"And I was left in the mines in my old age. I took you in like a son, Zippy. And you left me without a word," his dwarven friend Thograyn bawled.

This one brought Zippy to his knees. "Thograyn, I am so sorry. I should have told you. I did not know how to say goodbye, but I knew I could not be happy in the mines for the rest of my life. I had to leave, but I should have written you."

Cries crept in his ears from those he had left behind, and Zippy joined them. Soon the bog was to his waist, and he tried to fight against it, only to be pulled deeper with his sorrow. Tears streamed down his cheeks, and shame filled his chest.

"I'm sorry," he muttered.

And he truly meant it. He was sorry. Hurting the people in his life was never his intention, but he had to be true to himself. Nowhere had ever felt like home, and he could not settle into a life that felt like a lie. Still, this did not stop the guilt. He could have written, could have tried to stay in touch, to explain that him leaving had nothing to do with them, that he still cared for them deeply, but he did not. He hadn't made the effort, and the shame that lived in his nightmares was why. Their disappointment filled him with too much guilt to write.

Shame, guilt, disappointment, and fear consumed him. He could feel nothing else.

"Zippy, snap out of it," Blayne urged as he wrapped his arms around him. "Zippy!"

Zippy's eyes flew open to see the ghost of an elf smiling back at him with ominous energy. He turned to see Blayne trying to pull him from the ghost's embrace. "Be gone," Zippy yelled.

The forces still pawed at him, but he fought back. He remembered how many times he had told Razil to love herself regardless of her past. He deserved to give himself the same grace even as dishonor threatened to consume him whole. He took a deep breath and yelled again as he let go of the negative energy encasing him.

Blayne fell back at the release, and Zippy landed on top of him. They scrambled to their feet, and Dracklin ran to them, concern evident on his face. Dracklin extended his hand to both men and hauled them up from the watery peat. He brushed the mud from Blayne's cheek and pulled them forward to continue walking. Their pace quickened as they moved ahead into the dense vapor.

"Lyss!" Razil screamed from ahead.

Blayne picked Zippy up and ran after Dracklin, who began sprinting towards Razil's cry. Razil's screams were blood-curdling and terrified. Zippy had never heard her so hysterical. His heart hammered in his chest as he feared her fate.

When they got to her, Blayne dropped Zippy on the ground. He fell to his bottom on some dead plant matter and quickly scurried to his feet. Razil was on her hands and knees, a spirit grasping at her. The creature recoiled as if in pain when it reached her chest. Zippy realized her amulet protected her from the apparition's dark magic.

She was shaking a figure in the water. "Wake up!"

Dracklin attempted to help her grasp the person from the water. Together, he and Razil heaved with all their might until Alyssandra appeared from the bog, her eyes glazed over in a white haze.

The harder they tugged, the more fiercely the force fought against them. Its translucent frame was wrapped around Alyssandra's arms and legs, and it screeched in protest. Its arm reached from behind Alyssandra's chest, and Dracklin was pushed backward by the head, the sheer force of the blow rendering him unconscious.

"Drack," Blayne shouted as he rushed to Dracklin's side. He lifted Drack's head to cradle it in his lap.

"Zippy, I need your help," Razil cried, looking back with panic in her blue eyes.

Zippy rushed to her side. The ghost engulfing Alyssandra tried to grab him as he did. A cold sweat broke out along his back, but he pushed back at the fear. "What can I do?"

"Play a song. Maybe your magic can counteract this beast's power, and it will release her," Razil said as she continued to pull Alyssandra from the spirit.

Alyssandra's eyes were a milky white, and her body began to convulse under the ghost's grasp. Zippy wrenched his lute from his back in a frenzied tug. He began playing a jovial song loudly, directing it at the spirit. The spirit hissed and screeched at the magic as it filled the air. He played and played, but the spirit still held Alyssandra, though its grip had loosened. With a snap, the ghost lunged forward, striking Zippy backward, causing him to drop his lute.

Razil looked back at him with a pained look in her eye. "Zippy, check on my mother when you return to Gar Thanik."

"Razil, what are you doing?" Blayne blurted, rushing to his feet as Dracklin stirred and woke.

Time seemed to stop as Zippy watched what happened next. He wanted to intervene, but he was paralyzed, fear holding him in a tight grip, drenched in mud and seething in terror.

Razil lifted the amulet from her neck, the ghost lunging for her as she did. She fought against the spirit and pushed herself against Alyssandra, straining to place the amulet around Alyssandra's neck, who screamed in agony as charring skin appeared under the necklace's chain.

Razil grabbed Alyssandra's hand and wrapped her fingers around her saber before plunging the blade into her own heart. Alyssandra's screams dissipated as her eyes returned to their normal dark coloring. Razil's amulet gleamed around her neck, healing the burns. The ghost lurched away from Alyssandra almost painfully.

Razil fell to her back, and Dracklin rushed to her side, picking her up before the ghost could take her. Zippy's suspicions about the amulet's abilities proved true; the amulet was protecting Alyssandra now.

When Zippy looked at Razil's limp body hanging from Dracklin's arms, his head felt like it was floating outside his body.

"Run!" Dracklin roared horrifyingly as his chest heaved in and out.

Blayne lifted Zippy from the ground once more and ran, the watery ground splashing against his ankles. Alyssandra followed behind, her sobs audible. Zippy hung from Blayne's arms, sagging in disbelief.

Zippy's mind went blank as they ran until the wetness from the ground dried and the fog lifted. Dracklin gently placed Razil to the ground, the saber still impaling her chest with blood pooling around it.

Chapter 14

A Song of Soul

Zippy wiped his perspiring hands on his mud-covered doublet as he stared at his friend. Alyssandra knelt over her with tears streaming down her face. She tried to put the amulet back around Razil's neck, but it only burned Razil's skin. Blayne knelt at his cousin's side, placing two fingers on her neck.

His green eyes lit up. "There's a pulse. It's weak, but it's there."

Zippy placed his hand on Blayne's shoulder. "Once that saber is removed, she will bleed out and die in an instant. If the amulet believed she had a chance of survival, it would have never allowed Alyssandra to harbor it as its new owner. This is a dark magic, I fear."

"Ahhhhh!" Dracklin thundered as he threw his battleaxe across the grassland.

Alyssandra looked at him with tear-streaked cheeks. Her normal confidence was wilted as she drooped over Razil's body. "You have magic, do you not, Zippy? That is why people are always giving you coins. That's how you were able to avoid the cursed webs and make it to Hanni in the forest."

"Well. I. Umm..." Zippy stuttered at the accusation.

"Zippy, in the forest, you said yourself you are made for more. If anyone can do this, you can," Blayne pleaded desperately.

"Yes, I was taught magic through music from the Elvin wizard Malachi the Orange, who lived among the gnomes in Berry Meadows. But we did not spend extensive time in healing," Zippy said.

"Please try," Alyssandra begged.

Zippy was petrified. He never intended to use magic as more than a means to an end. A silly little melody to manipulate emotion when necessary and get what he needed out of a situation. It gave him a way to pay for his travels and placate an angry aggressor. He never thought he could do more, but then he remembered Hanni.

She had called to him, believing him strong enough in magic to sense her through the webs of wickedness laid by Wolf's wizard. She thought him worthy of more than a cheap trick, and he had believed in himself then. Now, it was time for him to do the same.

Zippy was silly and fun; this was true. But he was also more. He deserved more. He could give more. Not because he had to, but because it was woven into the very fabric of who he was. He was powerful and meant for more than swindling, running, and joking.

"Okay. I think I can stop the internal bleeding momentarily. But we will need to cauterize the wound immediately when the saber is removed," Zippy responded, his palms clammy. He had never been more determined to be successful or more afraid of failure.

"On it," Dracklin said as he started collecting branches from a nearby tree. "Blayne, help me."

Blayne ran after him and began grabbing dried leaves and twigs for kindling. Dracklin dug a small hole and lined it with rocks to avoid a forest fire, while Blayne placed kindling in the center. Dracklin struck his flint to spark a fire. Dracklin pulled the dagger from its sheath around his ankle and began heating it in the flames.

The blade turned an orange-red hue, and Zippy took a deep breath. He was going to attempt this. He had to. Razil had become an integral part of his life, and he could not imagine her not in it.

"Here goes nothing. If this goes well, I should be able to calm the cells in her body the way I do in peoples' minds. We will remove the saber while the cells are still and seal her with the heat. Then, we just hope she finds her way back to us when the bleeding stops." Zippy looked at Razil as he spoke.

Her body was dirty and her face was pale. Her skin looked clammy as grime and moisture collected on the blonde hair plastered to her forehead. He had never seen her so frail, and it sickened him. The person he loved most was on death's door, and despair threatened to overtake him; however, he could not allow it. She needed him now more than ever.

Zippy began strumming as he approached Razil's body. Alyssandra stayed next to her, holding Razil's hand as Zippy played his lute. Razil's body stirred, whimpers escaping her lips as Zippy began to sing.

> *Veins entwined in soul,*
> *Wrapping around her bones,*
> *Breathing life into her cells.*
> *Escaping, though you may,*
> *Stop your descent,*
> *Free her body from your seeping frame.*
> *Stunned, you seek to find,*
> *Her lifeblood once again.*

Razil's whimpers stopped, and her frame went rigid as if every muscle in her body stiffened in place. The blood seeping from around the saber in her chest stopped. Zippy smiled at her catatonic figure. His song had worked.

"Dracklin, now," Zippy ordered over his shoulder, hoping with every fiber in his being that this would work.

Dracklin and Blayne bounded toward Razil's limp frame. Blayne swiftly ripped the fabric around Razil's wound and removed the saber, leaving an opening in her chest that was not bleeding. The cells held still, as Zippy's fingers bled. He played with all his might, but Zippy knew he could not hold it this way much longer. Dracklin pressed the hot dagger against the gaping wound, and the skin cauterized. Burning flesh stung Zippy's nostrils, and he changed his tune to a more upbeat song with the last of his energy.

> *Awake, awake, awake,*
> *Daughter of the city,*
> *Awake, awake, awake,*
> *Death has left your body.*

Razil's body began to twitch, and her lips muttered incoherent sentences. She looked as though she was having a nightmare as her body became drenched in sweat. She convulsed and her eyes opened, then rolled back into her head.

"Please wake up," Zippy begged on an exhausted breath.

Blayne paced in silent dread as he stared at Razil's shuddering frame.

Alyssandra held her body down and whispered, "Razil, you are safe. Wake up, my love."

Alyssandra pulled back as the chain around her neck began to hiss. Red blisters formed where the protection amulet touched her neck. She screamed and pawed at it as she ripped it from her collar and threw the amulet to the ground, its black pendant shining.

Razil's blue eyes fluttered open, and a flush of red skin filled her previously lifeless cheeks. She looked side to side, and confusion took over her features. "What happened?"

Alyssandra slapped her on the cheek and screamed, "You died! You insufferable idiot. You died."

"It seems I am among the living," Razil said, placing a hand on her cheek. Her eyes looked weak and as if she might faint.

Zippy was reinvigorated at the sight and threw his lute on the ground and could not contain his hands from clapping and his feet from dancing. He grabbed the amulet and placed it around Razil's neck, though it burned him to do so. Her coloration normalized, and her eyes became more alert. The amulet continued healing her from within.

Dracklin threw himself on the ground and gently cradled Razil as he sat her upright. For a burly brute of a man, he had a soft spot for Razil. A single tear ran down his cheek, landing on her forehead. Blayne knelt and ruffled her sweaty hair, his features gone from silent shock to relieved.

Everything was quiet for several long minutes as they stared at their friend, who was still recovering. The fog was lighter but still floated over them eerily. The hair on Zippy's neck stood on end. The minute Razil could walk, he was ready to leave this forsaken place. When Razil's eyes returned to their normal blue, she looked around, questioning.

"You gave us a scare, friend. You almost met your end," Zippy explained. "Looks like the amulet rejected Alyssandra since she could not finish the act of your death."

A look of remembrance flashed across Razil's face. "Lyss, you were dying. I had no choice. I didn't think you'd care if I were dead after what I did."

Alyssandra huffed as she rose to her feet. She scoffed and said, "I do not care if you die."

Razil smirked. "Okay."

"Wipe that smile off your face. I am still very angry with you," Alyssandra said as she pouted her thick bottom lip. Razil looked wounded, and Zippy knew she would never forgive herself for what she had done to Alyssandra's father.

"Lyss, what were you doing in the bog?" Dracklin asked, crossing his bulging arms and raising an eyebrow. "I figured you would've traveled back to Gar Bladesin to recruit more members before trying to face the dragon by yourself. Walking the bog alone was a major risk. Had we not found you, you would have been dead."

Alyssandra looked at Dracklin and then averted her eyes. She blew out a breath and said, "That *was* my plan. But Wolf found me before I had the chance to make it to Gar Bladesin. He had me walk through the bog first to look for deep spots where ghosts lie before letting his rogues pass through."

Zippy gasped. "So, Wolf is ahead in this journey. My guess that he braved the bog was correct."

"We cannot let him beat us to the dragon. He would become an unstoppable tyrant if left to start his own city. And I fear his power would not end there. He will not be satisfied until he rules all of Gar. We cannot let him win," Razil said as she stumbled to her feet.

"We shall travel in the morning. For now, let us rest," Blayne said, looking at his cousin with concern.

"Yes, let us rest. We need our strength for the journey ahead," Zippy chimed in. "Alyssandra, will you leave us again? Please would you join us? We need your dragon blade, and you need the help we can offer as a unit. Also, I miss you, and Razil has been melancholy without you." His last sentence caused Razil to blush, her mouth opening and closing like a gaping fish.

Alyssandra looked at Razil and crossed her arms. Her eyes looked as if an entire war was happening from behind them. "I will join you; though, I still need time to process and forgive you, Razil."

Razil looked at her and nodded solemnly. "I do not expect your forgiveness. Even so, when we are successful, you should lead the land from the king's decree. I will return to Gar Thanik and live with my aunt and uncle again if that is what you wish."

The statement took Zippy aback, but he agreed. Alyssandra was more versed in politics, and it made sense for her to lead. But Razil should be a part of the city's conception. She, more than anyone, understood the city's difficulties and had insight on how to start a community that empowered people—all people, not just those with filthy wealth who prey on others to the point of their poverty.

Part of him worried that Razil's guilt was getting the best of her, and this was the primary contributor to her logic. Nevertheless, what he said previously stood true: They needed Alyssandra's dragon blade to stop Wolf successfully. Even without Razil, Alyssandra would be a far better leader than Wolf.

"I do have something to confess," Alyssandra said as she looked down at her hands.

"And what is that?" Dracklin asked.

"When Wolf captured me, he took Dragon's Bane and its amulet pair with him," Alyssandra said with misty eyes.

There was a moment of silence while everyone took in the heaviness of that statement. There was no killing the red dragon without a dragon blade, and to everyone's knowledge, Dragon's Bane was the last of that type of weapon.

"Then we track Wolf and slay him along with the beast," Razil said, her cool blue eyes fixed on Alyssandra.

"I'm in," Blayne pronounced as he patted Razil's shoulder.

"As am I," Dracklin chimed in.

"Then it's settled," Zippy said with a clap and a little side-step jig. "Tomorrow, our quest begins again."

Chapter 15

The Hunt

Blade Mountain could be seen in the distance; a day's journey at most. It had been weeks of walking and navigating through the rain and rugged landscape. The sun waned in the sky, and clouds formed from above. The air smelled humid, and the grass itched at Razil's calves.

She still could not believe she had died and been brought back to life by Zippy. He always joked and seemed like the life of the party. But Razil always knew that was a mask. She couldn't shake the vision of him at Hanni's cottage and the courage he showed. He was far more powerful than he led himself or anyone else around him to believe.

She touched the amulet dangling around her neck. It saved her life more than once, but it felt like a blight haunting her as it rested upon her tacky skin. It carved a hollowness into her heart that she endeavored not to dwell in. She attempted to shake the emptiness overtaking her chest as she continued walking.

The grassland stretched for miles before reaching the tightly pointed mountains. She wondered where Wolf and his travel party were. They lost their tracks a day or so ago when the grass became higher.

They trudged along, pushing straight through the terrain to reach the mountains. Hopefully, they reach the mountains first so they can have the high ground on Wolf to capture Dragon's Bane before reaching the dragon, but she feared this wouldn't be the case.

"We need meat—no more berries and breads. No offense, Zippy," Drack said as he looked over his shoulder at Zippy.

"No offense taken. I agree. The confrontation ahead is imminent, and we need a proper meal and sleep to meet tomorrow. But I know you will most likely eat rabbit, and I cannot, so I will stick to my berries and bread. Gnomes do not eat rabbits; we prefer berry pies," Zippy said with a light voice and bright smile.

"I forget about your rabbit god," Drack said as he ran his hand through his hair.

"I am not devout, but still, I cannot bring myself to consume the children of our deity, Zajac. Much in the way you would not kill a wolf even though you are exiled from your barbarian tribe," Zippy replied.

"I will hunt," Blayne offered. He had taken the crossbow from Wolf's ruffian who was eaten by the forest troll weeks prior. It had proved useful in killing rabbits.

"I will go with Blayne and help," Lyss said quickly, averting her eyes from Razil.

It was like a punch to Razil's gut every time she did this. Lyss seemed to take any opportunity to avoid being in the same vicinity as Razil. She understood Lyss' loathing, but it did not make it less painful. Excruciating even.

Without thinking, she announced, "I will go too. I fashioned a decent sling. I think that it will aid in the hunt." She hoped the last part would throw Lyss off the scent that she couldn't care less about hunting and just wanted to spend time with Lyss.

"I think I'm going to scout a place to set up camp instead," Lyss muttered, and she stomped off into the tall grass toward a cluster of sparsely leafed trees.

"Yikes," Drack said with raised eyebrows.

"Shut your mouth," Razil said as she punched his arm.

"She just needs space," Blayne interrupted.

"I know, Blayne!" Razil shouted. Her voice was much louder than she intended, and he winced. "Sorry, I do not mean to yell at you. I know she hates me, and I understand why. I would hate myself if I were her, too."

Zippy tugged on her sleeve, and she looked down into his gentle, round eyes as he stroked his long, red beard. "I do not think she dislikes you at all, Razil. I think that is why this is all so painful for her. Quite frankly, I think she feels the opposite of hate for you."

Razil scoffed and shook her head in disbelief.

"Maybe go and talk to her," Zippy insisted further.

"Couldn't hurt," Drack said, then slapped her back. "Besides, it's not like it can get any worse from here."

"Wow. Thanks," Razil replied, sarcasm dripping from her tongue.

"I meant that to be encouraging," Drack said as he shrugged.

She looked at all three men and trudged after Lyss without a word. Her heart was beating into her throat, and with every step, a hollow dread filled her stomach. She did not even know what to say. As she approached Lyss, the other woman did not turn around.

The hood of her black cloak was down, and her hair pooled down her back in thick waves. Her shoulders were hunched slightly, and Razil thought she heard a sniffle. Was Lyss, the fierce rogue, crying?

"Lyss, umm... I came to umm..." Razil stuttered but was cut off from finishing her miserable sentence.

"Have you no social sense? I came out here to be rid of your company," Lyss said harshly, but the watery sound in the back of her throat confirmed Razil's suspicions.

Something took over Razil's body, and this unnamed force pushed her feet to move in Lyss' direction. Blood surged through her body in waves, and Razil's throat went dry with fear. She should walk away and give Lyss her space, but step by step, she grew closer to the woman she could not get out of her head.

When she was a breath away, she inhaled. Lyss' light flowery scent that permeated from her hair filled Razil's nose and made her head dizzy with want. All she wanted was this woman. Be damned with the dragon and this fruitless quest. But she knew she did not deserve her. The one thing she wanted most, she would never and could never deserve.

Lyss turned to face her with red eyes and tears streaming down her cheeks. It took all of Razil's self-control not to wipe them away. She could not stand knowing she was most likely the cause. These past weeks had been torture. She missed their nightly talks in the forest. Missed the warmth that enveloped her when Lyss lay close and whispered dreams and nothings just for her to hear. She missed the way she felt when Lyss had her hands in her hair and her lips so close that Razil could taste her.

Razil went to speak again, but Lyss beat her to it.

"Go away, Razil," Lyss said through gritted teeth, but the anger did not reach her eyes. No. A deep pain settled in their dark brown depths.

"I will, I promise. I just wanted to say I am sorry," Razil said softly.

For a moment, Lyss stared at her. The air was sticky and hanging in Razil's lungs like a thick fog. She hoped the clouds would turn to rain to distract from this awkward conversation. What was she thinking, walking over here? She looked down at the swaying grass, waiting for

Lyss to break the silence because she had no idea what to say; she just wanted this tension to end.

"You have said that you're sorry already," Lyss responded. She continued staring at Razil. The eye contact was a nice change of pace, although Razil wished it held more affection than it currently did.

The sadness in Lyss's gaze turned to vitriol, and hate brewed in its place. Now, she looked like she had the night they met when Razil broke into her bedroom.

"Do you have a point of being here other than to hurt me further?" Lyss snapped as she motioned her hands in front of her.

Razil winced. She could hear Lyss' labored breathing and saw her shoulders tense. Regardless of her angry eyes, Razil knew this was deeper than hate—this was a broken heart.

Razil could see it now in the way Lyss' skin was flushed and her hands trembled. She loathed herself for making Lyss feel this way. She wanted to fix this so badly. Change her past so desperately.

Words formed in her throat and stopped there. Razil wanted to speak, but the words refused to leave her lips, so she placed a hand gingerly on Lyss' shoulder instead. Lyss shrugged her off, and Razil realized she was being inappropriate and turned to leave. She needed to respect Lyss' boundaries.

She took one step away before Lyss' shaky voice made her freeze, and she turned to face her once more. "I know you lived a hard life and had done horrible things in the past. I knew you were one of Wolf's top rogues, and with that comes more than petty theft. That's what makes me so angry. I just..." Lyss' voice cut off as tears streamed down her face.

This time, Razil couldn't help herself as she gently wiped them away. Lyss did not flinch or move away this time. "I knew you had done horrors, but I also knew that you were good, that your heart was pure. You did those things for survival, and they haunt you. I could feel your gentleness, your quiet boldness, your loyalty, and your way of seeing people to their core. And I let myself fall for you and grow an affection for you that I should never have. It makes me so angry because I want to despise you, but instead I..."

She didn't finish her sentence, and the following moments were something out of a desperate fever dream. Lyss' hands were on her waist, and she pulled Razil flush with her body. Razil could feel the swell of her breasts pushed against her as Lyss' chest heaved in and out. Before Razil could speak, Lyss' lips were crashing into hers.

It was not a gentle kiss. It was frenzied and frantic. Tears streamed down Lyss' cheeks and dampened their lips, and soon Razil's own collided into the watery mix. She could feel Lyss breathe into her and take her bottom lip between her teeth. Razil matched her pace and pressed deeper into the kiss, allowing Lyss' tongue to dance with hers.

Teeth. Tongue. Lips pressed hard against her own—rapid breathing. Lyss' hands running up and down her sides.

Razil could not think or rationalize. She was reduced to sensations and desire. Her brain was gone, and her body took over. Razil placed her hands in Lyss' hair and moaned as Lyss slipped her thigh between her legs. This is not how she pictured this happening. She imagined their first kiss to be tender and full of love and affection. Still, all she could do was feel and pray this was real.

Then all at once, it stopped. Lyss tore away from her without a word and looked at Razil with her dark and cutting eyes before walking back towards the men. Razil placed a finger over her lips, still feeling the ghost of Lyss' touch, trying to decipher if that was real or if she had just imagined it.

An uncomfortable throat-clearing caused her to look up. Blayne was standing with a crossbow in hand. "Still want to go hunting with me?"

"Huh? I mean... Of course. Yeah, of course we can go hunting," she responded. She looked at her cousin, whose face was very telling. He looked sorry for her, almost. Heat billowed along the base of her neck, and a nauseous feeling erupted in her stomach. "Umm... Did you see that?"

He shifted his gaze to the grass that matched his eyes, then back up at her. His expression was empathetic and knowing. "Did you want me to see that?"

She laughed awkwardly and wiped the stray tears from her eyes. Crying while kissing. That was a first. She hung her head and said, "Not particularly. I don't even know what that was."

He shrugged. "Then I did not see a thing." He paused for a moment before blurting out, "If it makes you feel better, I fancy Dracklin."

Her cousin's face was beet red, and he looked like he might die of embarrassment. He rubbed his hands together awkwardly and rocked back on his heels as he averted his eyes from hers.

Something about the admission and the awkwardness of his stance made her laugh. Razil laughed, and not a soft laugh, a hearty laugh that came from her stomach. Of course, Blayne fancied Dracklin. Who wouldn't?

"Wow. I knew I didn't have a chance, but I didn't expect this much laughter. Glad I made you feel better, I guess," Blayne muttered.

"Sorry, Blayne, I don't mean to laugh. That was just the last thing I was expecting you to say. But Dracklin is a great guy, and gay in case you were wondering. You would make a lovely pair, and you should go for it," Razil encouraged as she wiped tears of her previous laughter from her eyes. "I think you have a much better chance with him than

I do with Lyss," Razil added with a sad pang dropping back in her stomach.

"Really?" Blayne asked.

"Yes, really. It's making more sense to me why you joined this quest in the first place," Razil said as she jokingly pushed his shoulder.

"Well, that was one reason," Blayne said as he met her eyes again.

"Well, I may not admit things like this often, but I am glad you did," Razil said, and she meant it. Yes, he annoyed her, but it wasn't really him. Really, she envied his normal life and his constant goodness. She felt anything but. She was a perpetual mess, and she was beginning to realize more than anything, all she ever wanted was normal.

He placed her sling in her slightly unsteady hands. "You left this back there. Come. I think there may be some rabbit holes up ahead. Best to move before the day gets away from us. And I promise not to speak of either of our ill-fated love interests any further."

Razil twirled the sling in her hand and said, "Deal."

They walked and walked. Razil observed the ground, looking for rabbit holes. Her back became sweaty, and her mind was singularly focused. She was glad for the distraction and even happier that Blayne kept his word and didn't bring it up or bother her with his usual incessant chatter.

Razil's eyes scanned the ground as she walked low, tracking the area, until finally, she saw what she was looking for in the near distance. The ground gave way to a small hole burrowed in the grass.

"Blayne, look," Razil whispered, pointing ahead.

"Hey, umm... Can I say something? Before we start this whole rabbit business," Blayne said, awkwardly shifting his weight on his heels.

Razil did not like where this was going. "Sure," she responded skeptically.

"I am sorry," he said, green eyes drooping.

"You do not need to be sorry. It's not like you were spying on us or meant to intrude on my weird kiss. Plus, your news about Drack really did cheer me up," Razil said, trying to make him feel less awkward, even though she felt a burning feeling of confusion tearing through her chest at the thought of the kiss.

"No, not that. Though I am sorry to intrude on that as well," he said, then paused briefly before continuing, "I am sorry we did not take care of you as a child. That's the real reason I came. Yes, Dracklin is handsome, but more than anything, I want to make things up to you."

Razil felt a sudden jolt in her heart, and tears formed in her eyes. She was not in the mood for more feelings. "Blayne, stop."

"No. You were a child when your father died in the Orc Wars, and your mother shut us out. We thought she needed space to grieve. You were shut out as well in the process, and I know my parents regret not checking in more. We did not realize how bad it had gotten with your mom and what you had to do to survive. And that is on us. We should have been around and had your back," he said, barely taking a breath.

"Blayne, that's in the past. It is better not to dwell there," Razil responded, unsure of what to say, but knowing this was a wound she was not ready to reopen.

"I should have had your back. I should have been around. I should have noticed the squalor you were living in when your mother moved you to the Dim District. We did not know that the restitution from your father's death during the war went to your mother's addiction, but I should have found out. It was uncomfortable to be around the grief, so I put it out of my mind. But I should have had your back." He looked wounded, but then he continued, "It pains me to think of the poverty you must have faced there in the place where people go to die of starvation, exposure, or violence. The scar the city pretends does not exist. I remember seeing you pickpocket someone when you were thirteen and noticing Wolf's tattoo on your arm, thinking, what has become of my sweet, quiet cousin? And, I did nothing. It's so simple, the right thing to do. But I did not do it, and I am sorry."

Razil was stunned, and it took her several long minutes to respond. She did not blame her cousin for her childhood. If anything, she was just jealous of his. But she did not want him to carry the burden of regret or guilt. "You were a child yourself, Blayne."

He looked at her fiercely. A look not generally worn by him. "Still, I am sorry."

"I accept your apology," she finally responded. Then, she hit his shoulder. "Let's get some rabbits, you insufferable sap."

Blayne grinned widely, displaying his perfect teeth, and his eyes returned to their dopey green. At the sight, a little vine bloomed in her chest, stitching closed a wound she hadn't imagined would ever stop bleeding. She had a family, and they loved her. They knew her and they still loved her, even the parts of herself she tried to hide away.

Chapter 16

A Boulder and Wolf

For several days, Zippy and his party had been scaling the Blade Mountains ever so slightly so as not to alert the red dragon of their whereabouts. Zippy was exhausted by the slow, constant ascent up the thick rock encased in a prickly moss, navigating behind shrubbery and under trees as Crimshyrbane occasionally flew out, scouting his mountains.

Currently, Zippy sat on a rock shaded by a nearby tree with long, prickly leaves that was tucked neatly into the mountainside. The sun was high in the sky, and he was thankful for the shade.

"I think we should stay here until Wolf's thieving party arrives. We have a good vantage point, and are relatively hidden from Crimshyrbane's view," Blayne said as he plopped down next to Zippy and took a long swig from his water bladder.

"I agree. This is where we make our stand to regain Dragon's Bane from Wolf before entering the dragon's lair," Dracklin agreed.

Razil shrugged and said, "This is as good a spot as any if we are not already locked into a trap."

Though based on tracks, their party seemed to be ahead of Wolf, Razil was still reasonably skeptical. Even Zippy had to admit, it was almost too convenient.

Alyssandra did not add anything to the conversation, but Zippy was not surprised. She had been quiet and clearly lost in thought since they found her in the bog. He worried for her, but maybe once they acquired Dragon's Bane again, she would perk up. Though Zippy feared her solemn demeanor had more to do with a blonde rogue than any blade.

"I'll take first round scouting while you all rest," Blayne offered.

Razil looked over her shoulder at Alyssandra and said, "It's alright, Blayne, I got it."

She patted Blayne's shoulder, crouching as she slinked past their rocky cover, and moved to get a better view from below. Zippy was happy to see that at least the two of them seemed to be getting along better.

Alyssandra awkwardly fiddled with her hands until Razil moved out of view. Then, she came to sit by Zippy and Blayne. Blayne extended his water bladder to her, and she took a meager sip.

"I know she hurt you deeply. She is sorry, though, and she will never forgive herself," Blayne said as she handed him back the water.

Alyssandra ran a hand frustratedly through her raven black hair and said, "I know, Blayne."

Zippy truly felt her pain at that moment. It was obvious she cared for Razil deeply, but how could she forget that the person who killed her father was one and the same?

Zippy patted her hand, and she looked at him with teary eyes.

Zippy said, "You heal at your own pace. We are on this journey together, and when it is through, there will be time to figure this out with the land establishment in Gar. You do not have to forget or even forgive what Razil has done. I wouldn't blame you if you didn't. But Blayne is right—she has a good heart, even though she has done unpleasant things. Let us survive the next few days, and then we can figure this out."

Alyssandra took Zippy's hand and squeezed it. "Thank you, Zippy. Just a few more days." She paused momentarily and continued, "Who am I if I forgive her, though? A woman who dishonors her father's memory."

"Regardless of your decision, you are just a human doing your best to survive this world. None of us will judge or think less of you, no matter what is in your heart," Dracklin said as he walked over and leaned on the shade tree beside Zippy.

"How lovely." A dark, sadistic voice echoed, making them all jump.

Zippy peered towards the voice, and his heart beat hard in his chest. Wolf stood with a knife to Razil's neck. His grey eyes squinted in their direction as he smiled in satisfaction. The rest of his rogues appeared behind him. Zippy leapt to grab his lute, but it was too late. Wolf's wizard pinned him to the ground with a spell that felt like a rope tightening around his limbs, his blood flow slowing with the pressure.

Zippy gasped in pain. Dracklin charged towards Wolf and his rogues with Beatrice, Blayne following, hammer in hand.

Wolf stabbed his knife just deep enough for blood to spill from Razil's neck.

"Stop!" Alyssandra yelled. "He'll kill her."

Dracklin and Blayne jerked to a halt with frustrated snarls. Zippy tried to break his invisible bondage, but the harder he tried, the more painful it was.

"Forget about me! Get Dragon's Bane. He can't kill me with my amulet," Razil shouted as the wound on her neck began to stitch itself.

She grabbed Wolf's wrist, yanking it to the side as she headbutted him in the nose.

Wolf stumbled backward and dropped his knife. Razil tackled him to the ground and pawed at his waist for Dragon's Bane. Razil grabbed Dragon's Bane but was kicked off by Wolf before she could recover its amulet companion.

Dracklin and Blayne ran towards the commotion as Alyssandra ran to Zippy's side as he writhed in pain.

"Go help them," Zippy managed to say through pained whispers.

"I will not leave you," Alyssandra pleaded as she tried to place his lute in his rigid fingers. As hard as he tried, he could not play even a single note. Sweat beaded at his temples, and he feared he could not take much more.

Ahead, Dracklin growled as two rogues closed in on him. They swung rapidly with daggers, and Dracklin parried to keep from being stabbed. He was too overwhelmed to strike back. Blayne came to his aid, swinging his hammer and knocking the daggers from one rogue's hand, then following with a crushing blow to the temple. More rogues scurried towards them, and Dracklin and Blayne got back-to-back, blocking their blows. It was a fight to the death with swinging blades clashing with Blayne's hammer and Dracklin's battleaxe.

Razil continued to wrestle with Wolf, a true battle of stealth and strength. One would get the upper hand only to be cast down by the other. Dragon's Bane traded hands more than once until Wolf caught Razil in the side of the temple with an elbow, causing her to drop to the ground and release Dragon's Bane in the process.

"Now, Luther," Wolf shouted as he regained his footing. His wizard, wrapped in a black cloak, raised his staff in the air before thrusting his arms downward.

The ties around Zippy loosened as the ground began to shake. Dirt kicked up, getting in Zippy's eyes and sticking to his teeth. Rocks began to break and fall from above. Wolf and his rogues sprinted ahead. Blayne tried to follow but was hit by a small boulder as it came crashing down.

Dracklin lifted it from him as Blayne shouted out in pain. Zippy tried to play a song to stop their wizard from his current spell, but it was of no use. Wolf and his minions had already escaped, leaving a heap of rocks and boulders blocking their path.

Chapter 17

May I Have This Dance?

Hours upon hours of moving rock from the path had Razil's hands bleeding with sores, and her back felt like an ogre had stepped on it. Wolf's wizard had blocked the only real way up. The other part of the mountain was too steep to attempt, especially with Zippy.

The sun was slowly dying down, and Razil was thankful for the reprieve from its beams on her neck. Her body was drenched in sweat from head to toe. When she looked at Dracklin and Blayne, they looked the same, though Drack was trying to hide his exhaustion.

"Looks like you could use a break," Drack mocked over his shoulder as he pushed at an oversized boulder. He grunted in pain but tried to mask it with a cough.

"Looks like you need the break, barbarian of the desert," Razil sneered as she went to help him push. It barely moved, and Blayne joined. After lots of grunting exertion, it finally rolled to the side, revealing a slew of much smaller rocks.

"Looks like you're making progress," Zippy said from behind with a little cheer.

Razil looked over her shoulder and saw Zippy fanning his green hat over a small flame that Lyss seemed to have started using a flint. His cheeks were reddened, and he looked content despite their awful situation.

Lyss pretended she did not see Razil's gaze, which made Razil's chest feel sunken in.

"Why don't you all come take a break. Alyssandra and I almost have the fire started," Zippy said.

"Once we get this path cleared, we will," Blayne said, picking up more rocks and throwing them to the side. As much as Razil wanted a break, she agreed. This task had to be completed if they were ever to catch up to Wolf.

Rock after rock, Razil moved as the sun dipped beneath the horizon. Eventually, they finished, and a path was open for them to take in the morning. They could travel through the night, but Zippy thought it better to regain their strength before attempting to confront Wolf, or worse, the dragon.

Blayne grabbed a roasted piece of fruit Zippy had foraged earlier from a mountain shrub, plopped it in his mouth, and sighed. "This hits the spot. I think every muscle in my body is sore."

Drack raised his eyebrows and said, "Not me, I feel great."

"Is that why you are limping around like an old man?" Blayne asked sarcastically.

Lyss laughed as she scooted close to Zippy as he pulled out his lute. Her smile warmed Razil's heart. It had been absent for a while, and Razil missed it.

Zippy strummed a lighthearted tune, and Dracklin danced and shuffled his feet. "If I was sore, could I do this?"

"Oh wow. That's something," Razil joked.

"Well, I'd like to see you try," Dracklin said with an outstretched hand. Typically, Razil would deny such a request, but the lighthearted melody was a welcome distraction for the coming day and the awkward tension with Lyss.

Razil danced her heart out even as her muscles squealed in protest. Drack kept up step for step, and Blayne joined in, clapping his hands to the beat. Lyss stayed seated but watched them with amusement.

As Razil's limbs felt like they would give out, Zippy changed the song to a much slower tempo. The way the music bounced off the rocks made it feel sad, as if the music had somehow encapsulated how it felt to miss someone to your core.

Drack stopped dancing, his eyes cast downward. Razil's heart slowed as she listened, and she could not help but look at Lyss. Lyss' eyes looked teary, and she stood and walked off.

Razil went to go after her, but Blayne grabbed her arm and whispered, "Maybe just give her some space."

Drack ran his hand through his thick brown hair and said, "I say go after her. Maybe she'll listen."

Razil patted her well-intentioned cousin's hands, then followed after her. Mountain brush scratched against Razil's pants as she stumbled over various-sized rocks in the dark.

When she reached Lyss, her back was turned to her, and her shoulders were hunched. Sniffles and quiet cries escaped her as she stood in the distance.

"Why do you keep coming after me? I want to be alone," Lyss said in a watery tone.

A pang stabbed through Razil's chest at the sound. "I will leave you alone. I shouldn't have followed you. I just wanted to say I am sorry again, and I hate seeing you in pain. Especially knowing I am the cause."

Lyss turned around and threw her hands in the air. "I know you are sorry, okay? I get it, and I hate that I still talk to you. I should hate you, but I don't. I want to, but I don't. And what a dishonor that makes me to my family."

"You don't hate me?" Razil asked timidly. It made her feel slightly better, but not by a lot.

Lyss groaned in frustration and stomped over to stand in front of Razil. She took Razil's face in her hands and aggressively pulled her forward. Razil went to speak, but Lyss pressed her thumbs into her lips, silencing her.

"I love you, you idiot. And that makes me hate myself. What kind of monster loves their father's murderer?" Lyss screamed, her chest heaving beneath her maroon tunic. Her dark eyes became impossibly darker, and Razil hated how much she'd hurt this woman.

She loved her deeply, and a part of her leapt at the idea of Lyss returning her affection, but it was crowded by an equal amount of guilt. How could she love her after everything Razil had done? How could Razil love herself after everything she had done?

Razil muttered the only words she could think to say, "I'm sorry."

"You should be," Lyss whispered as she pulled away.

"What do we do from here? How can I fix this?" Razil begged. But part of her knew there was nothing to fix. The past was the past. An unchangeable force that made the present impossible to mend.

"What is there to fix? I love you, and I hate myself, and my father is dead. And to top it all off, I lost Dragon's Bane, and the tyrant is going to inherit a portion of the kingdom of Gar," Lyss said, seething.

"Yeah," Razil said as she looked at her feet. She wanted to scream to the treetops how much she loved her too, but it was as tainted as it was complicated. Both of them knew it.

"Yeah? That's all you have to say right now?" Lyss asked as she placed her hands on her hips in exasperation.

Maybe she should say how she felt. Razil was lost.

"I love you, too," Razil added, and was met with an annoyed groan. Razil felt utterly helpless.

Lyss pinched the bridge of her nose and sighed at the ground. Finally, she looked up and said, "You know what, let's put you and me aside. We have bigger issues. Tomorrow, we hunt Wolf and his rogues, then Crimshyrbane. After that, you and I can talk."

"That's fair," Razil said, her nerves calming slightly.

"That's more than fair. I shouldn't even be talking to you," Lyss said as she stormed back toward camp.

Razil followed her, but when they reached camp, her stomach lurched. The men were missing, and the fire had been extinguished. Razil crouched and saw hundreds of small webbed footprints and some broken animal bone weapons. It smelled of rot, and it appeared the men had been dragged based on the markings through the rocks and dirt.

"What happened here?" Lyss asked with a horror-stricken expression.

"Goblins," Razil said. "There are tribes that roam these mountains. We must follow with haste. If I am not mistaken, they may have taken them to sacrifice to the dragon."

"Crimshyrbane?" Lyss questioned.

"From rumors I have heard in the Dim District, certain goblin tribes moved to the mountains after the Orc Wars. Since many of their orc brethren had been killed in the war, they sought protection from the fabled evil dragons. The only thing is, they have to keep the dragon fed, which mostly means sacrificing their own. However, we just gave them the perfect meal," Razil said. "We must move quickly."

Lyss nodded, and they both stalked into the night, following the goblin tracks.

Chapter 18

THE KLIGEAUX

Goblins squabbled in their native tongue as black smoke filled the air around them. They danced around a large iron pot. Zippy's back ached from where it was tied to a large, pointy rock. He looked to his left and saw Blayne tied similarly with his hands behind him and his feet bound together. His eye was blackened, and his torso was bound by a thick rope to the boulder behind him.

Blayne was at least conscious. Dracklin was less fortunate and sat limp beside him, also bound. The trip here was brutal, and Dracklin's body had not yet recovered. Luckily, Zippy could see the gentle movement of his chest as it lightly rose and fell against his bindings.

They had had no time to react during the ambush. Zippy's lute had been torn from his hands before he could play, and clubs had been slammed against Blayne and Dracklin's skulls. Understanding he had little chance of winning on his own, Zippy faked a fainting spell. They were tied up and dragged by large boars with their goblin riders until they were brought to their lair and tied to these boulders.

Now, the morning light fought against the black smog of putrid fires.

Zippy could only hope that Lyss and Razil escaped a similar fate and would save them. As the light peeked through, he didn't see them, which gave him comfort that they were not captured as well. He just hoped they would find them before it was too late.

A goblin with wild black hair and pebbled green skin stalked towards Zippy with a rusty knife drawn. He licked his cracked lips, smelled Zippy, and looked like he might eat him right there. Zippy gasped in horror.

"No, no! You don't want to eat me. Gnomes are horribly gamey tasting. Perhaps a knight instead," Zippy squealed.

"Zippy, seriously?" Blayne shouted. The sound stirred Dracklin, and his eyes cracked open.

"Goblins?" Dracklin asked in a hushed tone. He tried to move but groaned in frustration as he slowly realized their predicament.

The goblin went to slice a hunk of Zippy's flesh, but was grabbed by another bald goblin with large facial piercings and thrust backward. He pointed at the sky and screamed at him in his native tongue. A thankful tear slid down Zippy's cheek.

"I wouldn't get too excited yet," Blayne muttered as he nodded his sweaty head toward the steaming cauldron.

The goblins continued dancing, waving their arms like wings and singing, "Kligeaux."

"That must be their tribe's name," Dracklin said.

A goblin with only one large tooth appeared with Zippy's lute and began playing. It was off-key and made Zippy's skin crawl.

"Careful with that, my green friend," Zippy pleaded.

The goblin rushed at Zippy and hissed, spittle jumping from its jowls.

"Okay, okay. You are doing great. Continue," Zippy said with a wince.

"Crimshyrbane! Kligeaux!" the goblins shouted against the morning sun as they waved their arms and danced around the cauldron.

"I think they're calling the red dragon," Blayne said.

"What?" Zippy shouted. The goblin hissed at him again, and a nervous fart escaped his cheeks.

"Calm down, Zippy," Dracklin whispered fiercely.

"How can we be calm when goblins are preparing to throw us in a cauldron to feed to the very dragon we are meant to slay?" Zippy asked in a panicked whisper.

Dracklin discreetly nodded towards Zippy's right. Zippy slowly turned his head and saw a hooded figure in all black. She stalked close to the ground, grabbed Dracklin's greataxe, and strapped it to her back. Blayne's hammer was already on her hip. She placed a gloved hand to her lips, signaling Zippy to be quiet.

Razil. Thank Zajac for Razil! But where was Alyssandra?

A whisper caressed his ear from behind the rock he was tied to before he could look further. "When the goblin turns, I will cut your bindings. Quickly make your way to Razil."

Dracklin coughed loudly and said, "This smoke is rotten."

The goblin holding Zippy's lute charged towards Dracklin and beat him over the head with it. Zippy's bindings loosened, but he could not escape without his lute. He stumbled and ran as fast as he could, grabbing hold of the lute as it was repeatedly smashed into Dracklin's skull.

"Give it here, you brute. You are going to destroy it," Zippy said as he grabbed and pulled at his instrument.

A loud snarl snatched his attention. The goblins stopped dancing and pointed at him. They ran towards him with crude animal bone clubs and minimal leather clothing. Finally, the goblin released his lute, but it was too late. The filthy beasts surrounded Zippy. Zippy tried to play a song, but it was so out of tune that it was no use. Zippy cowered in fear as the goblins swung their weapons at him.

He was saved by the slicing of an ax from behind.

"Zippy run," Dracklin yelled as he sliced through a goblin's sternum.

Zippy did not have to be told twice.

He ran towards the boulder, where Alyssandra stood holding two daggers. Blayne rushed past them to join Dracklin in fighting the beasts. Razil snuck into the fight, sliding her saber through the intestines of an unsuspecting goblin. The three fought ferociously, but there were so many of them.

A goblin scurried toward them, and Alyssandra swung a crude dagger that connected with the bone of the goblin's club. Bone splintered as she retracted and sliced at the goblin again with her dagger.

A growl from the sky shook the ground and temporarily stalled all the fighting. A huge dragon appeared in the sky, fire licking from its lips.

The goblins cheered, "Crimshyrbane!"

Dracklin, Blayne, and Razil took the momentary distraction to dart towards Zippy and Alyssandra.

"Let's go," Zippy pleaded.

Fire erupted from the dragon, scorching many goblins near the cauldron.

"Run," Razil commanded, and Zippy did not argue. He began running towards the rocks. Dracklin scooped him up and slung him over his shoulder.

Arrows whizzed past as they ran against the jagged ground. The dragon's roar bellowed in Zippy's ears, and he prayed to Zajac that the goblins would keep the creature occupied.

"Where are they?" Crimshyrbane questioned.

Goblins yelled, and large wings beat against the rocky ground from behind.

"We're next," Razil panted as she moved.

"There," Alyssandra cried out, pointing to an opening in the rock ahead. A foul smell leaked from the entrance, and the hairs on the back of Zippy's neck stood on end.

"I don't think we should go in there," Zippy argued.

"What choice do we have?" Razil asked.

Against Zippy's will, Dracklin ran toward the cave with the others. Crimshyrbane and the goblins stopped their pursuit at the entrance. That was a bad sign if nothing else.

Zippy blinked his eyes into the darkness, fearing they had just entered a greater threat than the one outside.

CHAPTER 19

THE CAVE

They should have listened to Zippy. There was something wrong with this cave. The air felt still. A quiet stillness that ended in death. Still, Razil trudged on through the darkness, following the only light, a torch held by Lyss up front. Razil chose to take up the tail to give herself some distance from Lyss and detect any enemies hiding in the cave that may try to ambush them. Her time with Wolf made her an expert at this.

"I don't like this," Blayne muttered, fear evident in his voice.

"It was this or death by dragon fire and goblin clubs," Dracklin replied.

"Does it not frighten you that not even the goblins would follow us into this place?" Blayne asked.

No one answered, but the dread sank deep into Razil's chest. He was right.

"I can't even play my lute to brighten the mood," Zippy said, breaking the silence. Razil squeezed his shoulder, urging him to keep moving.

Silently, they continued, trying to find an exit point. Occasionally, Lyss' torch flickered against the obsidian rock that surrounded them.

This place seemed to be the absence of everything, including color and sound.

Their steps sounded out of place in the nothingness surrounding them. Razil hoped Lyss' torch stayed lit. It was one of the only ones left in her supplies pack, and she did not want to be left in the dark.

"Surely there is a way out; if not, we wait until the goblins and dragon leave," Drack said.

"Agreed," Razil said, but an uneasy swoop squirmed in her stomach as she did.

Every second felt like hours as they slowly moved through the cave following Lyss' light like lost moths. Blayne stopped in front of Razil, causing her to bump into his back.

"What are you doing?" she asked, and Blayne turned around with his hammer in hand.

He did not respond and swung his hammer at her forcefully. Razil dove to the side, barely missing his blow.

"Blayne! What are you doing?" Razil screamed.

She scrambled to her feet and pulled her saber from her hip. He charged her, swinging his hammer rapidly. She parried, blocking his blows with her saber.

"Blayne, what is the meaning of this?" Drack asked as he grabbed Blayne's arms and attempted to pull the hammer from him.

Blayne headbutted him in the nose. A crack echoed through the tunnel, followed by the sound of dripping blood. He continued to swing at Razil, and she parried carefully, trying not to harm him in the process. This wasn't him. Something was controlling him.

Lyss ran over to him, swinging her torch in his direction. It illuminated his eyes, which had gone completely white. He didn't even have pupils, and the sight was disturbing. His face was shiny with sweat, and his nostrils flared.

"What the…" Lyss stuttered, but was cut off when he swung his hammer at her.

As he did, he turned his back on Razil. A translucent, grotesque-looking worm with a long red vein running through its center was clinging to his neck. It pulsed and seemed to be moving further into the back of his neck.

"There's some sort of worm controlling him," Razil shouted.

He turned towards her and started swinging again. Zippy tried to crawl up Blayne's back and pull it off, but he was easily shrugged off. Drack pulled him into a headlock and grabbed the thick worm the size of his hands as Lyss illuminated it with her torch. Blayne thrashed and screamed in protest until Dracklin removed the worm from his neck, revealing needlelike teeth covered in blood. Drack shrieked in terror and threw it at the wall.

Blayne fell to his knees. Zippy picked up his drooping head. "Are you okay?"

"I think I may…" Blayne started but then gagged, spitting bile from his mouth.

Lyss carefully approached the wriggling worm and burned it with the torch. It shrieked and writhed until it became charred and rigid.

A wet dripping sound from the wall drew Razil's attention. It sounds like something pushing against a wet sack. The hairs on the back of Razil's neck stood on edge.

"I hear something by the wall," Razil said. She walked towards the sound, and Lyss followed behind with the torch.

When they reached the wall, the torch revealed a large purple sack that seemed to be pulsing like a heartbeat. Fear radiated through Razil's spine. Razil placed one finger on it to try and identify what it was, but as she did, the sack ruptured. Worms burst forward, covering Razil's torso.

She yelled and ran around in a circle. Drack grabbed her by the shoulders to still her.

"Get them off of me!" Razil shouted. Her skin prickled with gooseflesh, and her stomach roiled.

Lyss swatted at the worms with the torch, and Zippy hit them with his hands. They fell off her torso, but the worms were not held at bay for long.

From the sack, more worms came. They twisted and leapt at them. Razil stomped and swung her saber, trying to fend them off.

"We're surrounded! Run," Drack bellowed as he helped Blayne to his feet and began running deeper into the cave.

Razil followed, Zippy and Lyss behind her. She frantically ran her hands all through her hair and over her body as they moved. She felt like the worms were still all over her, even when Zippy assured her they were not.

Finally, when no more worms were in view and it seemed none were chasing, they stopped. Razil took stock of herself to ensure no more worms were on her. She needed more assurance than just Zippy's words.

Thankfully, none were attached to her person. She knelt against the hard rocky ground and caught her breath. The cave walls seemed impossibly darker but somehow more charged, like an invisible energy drew them in.

"I am sorry," Blayne said, looking down at the hammer now secured in his belt.

"You have always been a pain in my neck. Don't sweat it," Razil teased, but truthfully, she was still afraid they weren't out of the thick of danger yet.

"Does anyone else hear that?" Zippy asked.

"Hear what?" Drack asked with his battleaxe drawn. He looked more on edge than usual in the dark.

"The incessant buzzing sound. Like a siren song," Zippy replied.

"I hear it too. Something feels alive," Lyss said as she moved towards the cave wall with her torch. She knelt and ran her hands over the black rock.

The cave seemed to huff in protest, and the sound got louder. Lyss withdrew her hand and looked back at the others.

"I hear it too," Razil said as she approached Lyss. A buzz. A whisper. Something called to her from behind the wall of the cave.

"I knew I heard something," Zippy said.

"I don't like this," Drack replied.

Zippy joined Lyss and placed his palm against the jagged rock wall. As he did, a bright green light erupted from behind his hand. Rock crumbled and squelched as it fell to the ground.

"Zippy, look out!" Drack roared, but Zippy remained planted as rock continued falling from the wall.

Zippy was unafraid, and the cave seemed to welcome him even as it broke apart. As it fell around him, it seemed to disintegrate into ash. Soon, a door with a green light emitting from its entrance replaced the once dank cave wall.

Razil approached and ran her fingers around the cool gray stone chiseled with symbols and pictures. It appeared to be some archaic language long lost to time along the border of the door. She shifted closer and felt a gentle warmth coming from the light within.

"What is it?" Blayne asked as he came to stand behind his cousin.

"I have no idea, but I don't think it means us any harm," Razil said. The warmth from the door did not seem evil; instead, it seemed the opposite.

"I would not be so sure," Drack said, staying carefully behind, the ax still in hand.

"I think it is a portal of sorts. I feel the song of other lands coming from behind," Zippy said.

"A portal to where exactly?" Lyss asked.

"I believe a portal to where we wish to go," Zippy said.

"How can we be so sure?" Drack countered, taking a step closer to them.

"I am not," Zippy said.

Razil took a deep breath, calculating her options. She knew going back towards the worms wasn't one. And if they kept moving, who knew how long they would be trapped in this cave until they ran out of food and water? But was this mysterious door a viable option, or would it lead to death? Unfortunately, this question could only be answered in one way, given the lack of alternative options.

"I'll walk through," Razil said, stepping closer to where the gentle heat almost felt inviting. It tingled against her skin, raising the hairs on her arms.

She went to take another step, but was stopped by long, soft fingers wrapped around her wrist. Razil turned to see Lyss' face illuminated by the green light from the door. Her eyes looked impossibly dark, and a tear threatened to escape them.

"It'll be okay," Razil whispered as she leapt through the door before anyone could stop her.

Chapter 20

A DOOR OF DARKNESS

Zippy watched as his friends jumped through the stone doorway with apprehension. Humans were less educated in myth than gnomes, but they stepped through nonetheless. One by one, they disappeared through the green, humming light as if they had evaporated. Zippy stood still, not from fear—the opposite, really.

The green glow from the door settled around him like a blanket of light. He assumed it was a portal. Many tales had been told of them at Berry Meadows. Portals revealed themselves to worthy travelers in their greatest time of need, but most would never be fit to see one. He should be afraid—and of this cave he surely was—but the portal wasn't the same. It beckoned him like an embrace to step through, and that was why he couldn't move.

He didn't trust this feeling. He had felt it so many times before—an out.

This was his out, a way to flee without a warning. But he wouldn't. He would imagine the Blade Mountains and hopefully join his comrades at the other end. So, Zippy took one step forward, then another, until he could feel the door's energy envelop him.

His boot touched the light, and the rest of him was sucked through the entrance before he could step back.

Light of every color surrounded him. Shades he had never seen. It was the most beautiful and magical place Zippy had ever been. Starlit schemas fluttered around his eyes and surrounded him as a gentle whooshing sound entered his ears.

He tried to imagine the Blade Mountains, but was it truly what he wanted? Surely this was a portal, so it would bring him where he wanted to go if he chose it. But that was the problem. Zippy rarely knew where he actually wanted to go.

"Where do you wish to go?" a gentle voice asked from behind him.

Zippy turned to find a fairy with large auburn wings flapping against the starlit colors surrounding them. Her hair was the color of lilacs, and her skin glowed a gentle brown hue illuminated by a constellation of freckles. She was the most beautiful thing Zippy had ever seen. Her movements were a painting, and her eyes were the song of the deadliest siren.

"Where do you wish to go?" she asked again, this time more impatient.

"Who are you?" Zippy asked, awestruck. He had heard of portal fairies before. They granted you safe passage wherever you wished in Varki, but he had never imagined meeting one. He thought these portals were a myth.

"That is neither here nor there. The present is only where you wish to go," she said, and as she did, her lilac hair swam around her head like a serpent.

"Blade Mountain," Zippy said, but his voice faltered.

"A proclamation without conviction is a death sentence. An unsure heart shall remain in limbo, and my patience is thin. So, I ask you once more. Where do you wish to go? Do not answer unless you are sure," the fairy said. Zippy could feel her spirit begin to pull away from him as she did.

He feared that if he did not answer truthfully, she would do as she said, leaving him here to rot in this portal, in a purgatory of indecision.

"I just need a moment," Zippy begged.

"And a moment of truth I can give," the fairy said.

And truth, the deepest truth that can only come from one's soul, was what he was left to face. He knew what the right thing was. The right thing would be to aid his friends in their quest to find Wolf and reclaim Dragon's Bane before facing Crimshyrbane.

But then what? Where did that leave him after all this was said and done?

Surely, he would be expected to be a part of their portion of Gar as a founding member. And with that would come some permanence. And that was what scared him.

Disappointing his friends and leaving now would be a softer blow than leaving after this quest. They may think he didn't survive the portal, not that he'd left them when they needed him most. But how could he leave these people he had grown to love as his family?

But how could he stay? Staying was not who Zippy was.

"You fear your friends could not love your true nature," the fairy said, more of a statement than a question. She looked at him as if she could see past his flesh and into his spirit.

"Who could?" Zippy asked, fiddling with his hands.

"That is up to you," she said indifferently.

This opened up the darkest parts of him. The fear of never being enough, never being understood. He tried to fight back against it, but sweat beaded at the base of his neck. This indecision, this insecurity, it threatened to consume him.

"Do you know that your friends would expect out of you what you cannot give?" the fairy asked, tilting her head.

"I do not know that they wouldn't." Zippy replied, getting creeped out further by how deeply she seemed to be in his head.

"Then choose for them as you always do," she said.

"But maybe they'd understand. Maybe I could be in Gar Razil, or whatever they name it, under my terms," he wondered out loud.

"Then trust their love for you will accept you as you are. Love is a free thing. It accepts us and allows us to live in our way without expectation of rigidity," the fairy said.

Zippy pondered this with excruciating detail over and over. His friends did love him. They would accept him, allowing him to live on his own terms without judgment, to come and go as he pleased, and to love in his own way. But the question was, did he love himself?

Finally, he realized that he did and deserved to. He was not a flake or a joke. He was Zippy Redbeard; his friends would never defeat the dragon without him. A pride that felt like a much-needed hug swelled in his chest.

"Send me to Blade Mountain," Zippy said, and this time he meant it.

CHAPTER 21

ZIPPY REDBEARD

Razil was undone—truly undone. The rest of her party had been spat out of the portal and onto the rocky ground of Blade Mountain a lifetime ago. At least it seemed like a lifetime to Razil, but still no sign of Zippy.

Razil paced, her feet dragging against the pebbled surface as she bit at her already short fingernails. What could have happened? Surely Zippy knew they all imagined the same place. Surely the door would bring him here as it did everyone else—still nothing, as the sun beat against Razil's neck brutally.

"We need to leave," Drack said, but there was no conviction. Blayne nodded behind him, and the sight made Razil's skin crawl.

"We can't leave," Razil objected as she turned to face the gigantic man with pouted lips.

"Razil, I love him as much as you, but we can't wait forever. We must find Wolf and regain Dragon's Bane if we have any hope of defeating the red dragon," Drack said, almost begging.

"If you cared about him, you wouldn't even suggest it," Razil said with a cruel bite to her tongue.

Drack raised his arms to argue more, but before he could speak, Lyss cut him off and said, "Let's take a breather."

Her gentle fingers wrapped around Razil's forearms and pulled her towards the sparsely placed bushes away from Drack and Blayne. Razil went to protest, but simply couldn't. She knew the last thing she needed was to engage in a screaming match with Drack because, unfortunately, she knew he was right. Time was of the essence, and they could not wait forever.

They stopped when they reached the rough bushes wrapped in prickly brown leaves. Razil picked a branch off one and rubbed the papery leaves between her fingers as she refused to meet Lyss' eyes. It was all too much.

"Hey," Lyss said as she gently placed her hand on Razil's cheek. "Look at me."

Razil looked up... and she was not ready to face her. The love of her life and her greatest regret. She knew they were doomed because of her past, but she also knew she could never love someone the way she did Lyss. She just got her in a silent and knowing way.

As she looked at her with misty, dark eyes, her mouth slightly open to where the small gap in her front teeth was evident, Razil's heart jerked and leapt in her chest. Lyss didn't remove her hand from Razil's cheek, and heat seemed to billow underneath her touch. Razil sucked in a breath, tears fighting to escape.

"You can cry if you need to," Lyss said, stepping closer. Her breath smelled sweet, and her cheeks were stained with silent tears. "I cared for him, too, and I know it seems impossible to leave. But we cannot wait much longer, or we will miss our chance. We will find him after."

She knew Lyss was right, and her words finally brought tears to Razil's eyes. Not in the silent way they streamed from Lyss. Hers were fat, hot tears heaving from her eyes and bringing snot out of her nose like an uncontrollable stream. Lyss pulled her close, and Razil rested her face in the crook of Lyss' neck until her eyes shed no more tears.

She pulled back, embarrassed, when she regained composure. Razil wiped her nose on the sleeve of her cloak in the most unattractive manner.

"Sorry, I shouldn't have used you for comfort after everything I have done to you and your family," Razil said, her throat raw from sobbing. She was sad about Lyss, and she was gutted about Zippy. Everything was too much all at once.

Lyss grabbed Razil's cloak and fisted the dark fabric on her chest aggressively.

"Shut up," she said, then leaned in and kissed Razil, lips wet with tears and painfully soft.

Razil froze for a second, but it did not take long for her to match Lyss' hunger, both of them giving in to their feelings. It was a relief. Something that felt good amongst all the bad. They stayed like that for a while, kissing, crying, and kissing some more, saying everything without saying anything.

Finally, Lyss pulled back and said, "Razil, we have to go. We can't stay like this."

"Can't we?" Razil asked, her heart torn between wanting and grief.

Lyss slipped her hand from Razil's cheek and grabbed her hand, intertwining their fingers. She gently tugged and walked through the bushes back towards Drack and Blayne. Both men stared at them, clearly sad, but not saying anything.

"Drack, you're right. We need to move. We will find Zippy after this mess," Razil said as she squinted against the sun.

Blayne shuffled his feet against the tan colored rocks and nodded. He turned and started to walk. Drack huffed in a breath and followed him up the steep path towards the dragon's lair.

Razil looked to the sky and whispered a gentle promise, "I'll be back for you."

When she turned to follow the men, the air began to buzz with a static charge. Green light erupted from blue skies, and from it Zippy was propelled forward, rolling against the rough ground.

Zippy stood, brushed himself off with one hand, and held his seemingly repaired lute with the other. His red beard wrapped around his face like a halo, and his doublet was covered in mountain dust.

Razil had never been happier to see Zippy in her life. Her whole body felt lighter looking at her friend. From behind her, she heard a full body sigh of relief emanate from Drack. She knew he felt the same.

Razil ran towards him and wrapped him in a tight squeeze that lifted his feet off the ground. Drack and Blayne were soon at her side, ruffling his already messy hair.

"Miss me?" Zippy asked as they dropped him to the ground.

"More than you know," Lyss answered.

"What took you so long?" Blayne asked as he wiped away a silent tear of reprieve.

"You know I like to make an entrance. Now, let us go. We have a dragon to defeat," Zippy said as he played a triumphant chord on his lute.

"To Crimshyrbane's lair," Razil echoed, and as she did, she felt a small beat of hope.

Chapter 22

AN UNLIKELY PACT

Blade Mountain swapped between steep inclines and gradual slopes. Most of the mountain was covered in interspersed trees and prickly bushes, along with rough boulders. However, this close to the top, the foliage was minimal, and rocks covered most of the surface. They had finally reached Crimshyrbane's lair.

Crimshyrbane's lair was dark and jagged. It went deep into a cave at the top of Blade Mountain. It was easy to find, with the ground littered with goblin bones, but there was no sign of Crimshyrbane.

They had spent the previous day searching for Wolf and his pack of rogues, but there was no trace of them on the mountain except for occasional boot prints. All signs pointed to this cave, which was unusually quiet. The kind of calm that chilled bones and began nightmares.

Razil crept through the cave, careful not to be heard against the dark staleness of her surroundings. Wolf's absence disturbed her. Surely, she should have run into him by now based on the prints at the mouth of the cave.

It could only mean a couple of things. Wolf killed Crimshyrbane, and he now lay dead, or Crimshyrbane killed Wolf and his rogues. Razil did not know which she feared more.

She had volunteered to scout this cave alone, searching for clues on how to proceed. She hated to admit it, but she wished she had another watching her flank. Nonetheless, she would not let the fear overtake her. They were as good as dead if they did not recover Dragon's Bane, so Razil crouched low to the cave's floor, checking every nook for the blade and amulet as she shuffled deeper into the lair.

She was vigilant not to make a sound, taking each step carefully to avoid crunching on the bone of a goblin or kicking a loose rock. If Crimshyrbane was alive, she did not want to be caught without the weapon that could equalize the fight. Even with her protection amulet, she was unsure it would protect her long against the fire from a dragon's breath. And if Wolf's rogues were here, she did not stand much of a chance alone either. One of them would just need to hold her long enough that Crimshyrbane could consume her in his flame.

So, Razil snuck deeper and deeper into the darkness. She stilled her breath as she moved, her body lithe and traveling at a pace where even the most attuned ear would not hear. The cave seemed to go on and on until finally, she heard muffled voices from around the corner.

Light illuminated the darkness in a fuzzy glow, and its flicker hurt Razil's eyes as she adjusted from the utter darkness. She stilled, her heart pounding rapidly in her chest. The voices meant Wolf and his team. But then she heard what sounded like wings beating.

She moved so slowly that her bones ached. Finally, she was close enough to hear it.

Wolf's deep, sinister voice barked, "Faster, you idiots. We need him to have his fill to garner his full strength."

His fill? It made her skin crawl to think of what that most likely meant. Razil crept along the ground to see what was going on. Finally, she reached the corner and tilted her head to peer around the sharp rockface.

Flames erupted high towards the cave's ceiling as Wolf's rogues hoisted goblin bodies on wooden stakes, seemingly to roast them. Razil's breath caught in her lungs when she saw Wolf standing tall with his grey eyes piercing as his minions worked. He appeared to be on some kind of perch with straw and other assorted fabrics—perhaps the resting place of the red dragon.

From behind him, Crimshyrbane appeared from the shadows before she could ponder more. He licked his large, red lips, and his eyes narrowed like a serpent's. Her stomach roiled at the sight. No matter how many times she saw the dragon, terror raced through her.

"Yes, I will need my fill if we are to take over Gar," the red dragon said with a laugh. As he did, fire fizzled from his lips in little flashes.

"And if we don't want to follow you?" one of the rogues holding a limp goblin's body asked.

Crimshyrbane turned his massive scaly head, and without a word, fire spewed from his mouth, engulfing the man. He turned and looked at Wolf. Wolf looked afraid for the first time in his life as sweat beaded down his bald head. Nervous sweat formed similarly down Razil's neck at the sight.

"Work, you scoundrels. Crimshyrbane will be king of the land, but we will reap the benefits of gold. Do not defy me or the dragon again unless you want to end up like him," Wolf said as he pointed at the charred man with an equally charred goblin body splayed out on top of him.

The red dragon laughed and shifted back to sit on his haunches. As he did, Razil saw it. The ugly necklace she discovered so many nights ago in Alyssandra's room shone brightly, with its twin blade beside it. They rested under him on dry, yellowed straw.

Razil had heard enough. Wolf had joined Crimshyrbane and planned to exploit the dragon's strength to take over Gar. No doubt he would try to double-cross him later after they pulverized the land, though it seemed Crimshyrbane had control of Dragon's Bane for now.

Razil fled as quickly as she could without alerting them to her presence. She descended through the dark cave until she met her team at the entrance.

They stood there expectantly as she emerged.

Drack approached her and asked, "What did you find, friend?"

"Wolf and his rogues have joined Crimshyrbane. They plan to take over Gar," Razil blurted.

Quickly, she recounted everything she saw and heard in as much detail as possible. Lyss chewed her bottom lip as Razil spoke. Blayne tried to interrupt several times, but cut himself off to hear the rest. Finally, Razil stood there, out of breath and trying to formulate any semblance of a plan.

Blayne swung his hammer until the hilt landed in his hand. "What do you suggest, Razil?"

It was nice that her cousin trusted her now, knowing stealth was her forte more than his. Drack crossed his burly arms, waiting for her answer as Blayne held his weapon nervously.

"Lyss and I will sneak in and steal Dragon's Bane," Razil said. Lyss nodded as she said it.

"How do you plan to do that?" Drack asked skeptically.

This next part made her sick as she said, "We will need a distraction."

"And a distraction we shall be," Zippy asserted, his cheeks somehow jolly in the most unjolly of times.

"A distraction we shall be indeed," Blayne echoed.

Razil did not like it, but it seemed like their only hope. They could not leave now and let Crimshyrbane and Wolf take over Gar. It was now or never.

Blayne, Drack, and Zippy needed to distract the red dragon and his new allies long enough for Razil and Lyss to procure Dragon's Bane and kill Crimshyrbane with it. It seemed like a long shot, but it was the only shot they had.

CHAPTER 23

CRIMSHYRBANE

Zippy gripped his lute tightly as he pressed his back against the cold, sharp rock of the cavern wall. The faintest light peeked from around the corner. It was just enough to see Razil's piercing blue eyes from under her black cloak.

Any moment now, Razil would give the signal as she and Alyssandra slipped into Crimshyrbane's lair. Then it would be go time. Dracklin, Blayne, and Zippy would have to cause a big enough ruckus that Razil and Alyssandra would go undetected.

Zippy's stomach was a ball of nerves, as sweat glistened on his forehead even in the cave's coolness. His only consolation was that the portal fairy had fixed his lute before spitting him out on Blade Mountain. At least he would have his magic.

But could his magic compare to Wolf's wizard?

It would have to, or they wouldn't stand a chance.

Razil tapped her chest twice, and Zippy swallowed down the fear threatening to consume him. He darted around the corner into Crimshyrbane's lair with Dracklin and Blayne close behind.

The light source came from the flames engulfing charred goblins stacked one on top of the other on wooden stakes. Their green flesh oozed yellow pus as flames licked around their bodies. Crimshyrbane crunched his teeth around the bodies three at a time from a stake at the far side of the room as hooded figures watched in disturbed awe.

The putrid smell of the bodies was enough to knock Zippy out, but instead he played a chord of his lute and announced, "Well, this isn't the pub."

Dracklin propped his ax against his shoulder and said, "Silly us, anyone know the way to the nearest tavern?"

"I thought a cave would be an odd place for a drink, but Zippy normally has a knack for finding a good beer," Blayne said.

Crimshyrbane dropped the goblins from his mouth, and they fell with a bone-shattering thud.

"Who dares step into my lair?" he bellowed as smoke curled from his nose.

"They are the ones sent to kill you, master," a cloaked figure snarled as he moved to stand next to the dragon.

"Then deal with it. Prove your worth to me," Crimshyrbane said as he turned to finish his disturbed meal.

Wolf pulled back his hood, revealing a bald, scarred head. "Kill them," he ordered the others.

The wizard soon showed himself and attempted to conjure a hex. Zippy played his lute in his direction, and his magic seemed to freeze the hex in place. He pushed protection magic into every chord, and he sang not words but pained yodels as he held the wizard's magic at bay.

Between his songs, he shouted at Dracklin, "Go, I can take him."

Dracklin and Blayne ran towards the oncoming rogues. Daggers flashed in the firelight, but they parried easily with their respective weapons.

Blayne swung his hammer at a shorter, cloaked figure and connected with the rogue's skull. The man fell like a sack of potatoes. Wolf's attention snapped to the knight, and he charged Blayne, swinging rapidly at him with his daggers.

Blayne stumbled and fell from the speed of Wolf's attack. Wolf stalked toward Blayne but was stopped by Dracklin's ax as he swung at his torso.

His friends fought with ferocity, but he feared he couldn't hold the wizard's magic much longer. It wove into his own like a sickness. It leached the power from his notes and killed it, chord by chord. His confidence from before was waning.

Zippy played till his fingers bled and then played some more. He had to keep the wizard's magic from hurting his friends, but it was so intense he didn't know how much longer he could hold on.

From the corner of his eye, he saw Razil climbing a rockface toward a straw bedding structure. It must have been where Dragon's Bane was hidden. He just had to keep Crimshyrbane and Wolf's rogues occupied long enough that she could procure the weapon. She needed him.

He could do this. He had to do this. Once and for all, he decided to be the gnome he was always meant to be. His confidence returned, and he poured every bit of it into his magical music.

Blood dripped from Zippy's hands as he played harder and harder, until something amazing happened. His magic was no longer being consumed by the other. He felt the shift like a tide returning to the shore.

He was no longer on the defensive; he had taken control.

He marched forward, playing with such fervor that he could think of nothing else. Wolf's wizard staggered backward at the force of his lute's magic. The evil wizard's staff split, wood splintering around him as Zippy's song continued. He sank back and his hood fell back, revealing red eyes and a grizzly blond beard. The man's flesh was pulled so taut to his face that it looked like the bone might peek through.

He struggled to his feet, but it was too late. Zippy yelled a song so strong it ripped through his stomach and out of his mouth in a fury that felt like vengeance. The man gasped as the song tightened around his lungs until he took his last breath.

Zippy dropped to his knees and wept, for he had nothing left in his system to give, and he had taken his first life. He wiped his eyes with blood-smeared hands and placed his lute on his lap.

"Zippy, watch out," Blayne shouted, and Zippy turned his head to see Wolf charge him from behind.

His grey eyes narrowed on him like sinking stones as he swiped his dagger at Zippy. Zippy rolled to the side, avoiding the blade. He didn't mean to do it, but his eyes darted to Razil once more, hoping that if he died, at least his friends would be successful.

Wolf followed his line of sight and was gone before Zippy could recover. Zippy cursed himself. He gave away his best friend's location. His stomach curdled at the thought.

Before Zippy could do anything, Blayne was at his side, fighting off a cloaked figure who wielded a short sword and looked like a rogue Razil had called Deelaz Red at a previous encounter.

"I am so depleted. I have nothing left to give. Nothing left to fight," Zippy cried.

"Then let your friends fight for you," Dracklin said as he came to guard Zippy's other side.

Crimshyrbane finished chewing the goblins and looked around the room with disdain. Fire erupted from his jaw, and he burned the rogues fighting in front of Dracklin and Blayne. The rogues screamed and clawed at their bodies, which were consumed by the flame.

Crimshyrbane laughed, and fire erupted toward the blackened cave's ceiling. He pointed his head down and looked at them.

"You three are mine, and I shall enjoy killing you slowly," the red dragon said as he narrowed his serpent-like eyes at them.

Zippy picked his lute up from the ground and prayed to Zajac that he could find the strength to fight once more.

CHAPTER 24

THE HEIST

Razil climbed the rockface rapidly with Lyss in tow to snatch Dragon's Bane from Crimshyrbane's lair. She knew she must work quickly. The others could only distract the dragon and the rogues for so long.

When they reached the top, Dragon's Bane was not immediately visible. They must have hidden it. Lyss and Razil dropped to their knees, frantically pawing at the bloody straw and brittle bones scattered among the black jagged rock. If her friends died because of her incompetence, she would never forgive herself. She searched and scoured in a frantic blur.

The panic was not helping. Razil took in a deep breath and focused. She scanned the surface until a bump under a bloodied piece of straw drew her attention. She crawled over to it and moved the straw. The ugly red jewel revealed itself.

The necklace was wrapped neatly around the blade, and both gleamed their hideous red. Her spirits lifted at the sight, and she felt like a weight was lifted off her chest. Razil scooped them up and ran over to Lyss, who was still searching.

She tapped her shoulder and held out Dragon's Bane. "I found it," she whispered.

Lyss smiled from ear to ear as Razil dangled the amulet and dagger in front of her. Finally, Dragon's Bane would be wielded by its intended family line. Tarick and Hanni would be happy.

As Razil went to wrap the necklace around Lyss' neck, fear took over Lyss' features as she screamed, "Razil, watch out."

Razil turned to see Wolf racing toward her with a drawn blade. She tossed Dragon's Bane at Lyss and pulled her saber from her hip to face Wolf.

"Go, I will take him. You must slay the dragon," Razil shouted.

A moment of hesitation washed over Lyss before she slipped on the necklace and held the blade firmly in her hands. Wolf attempted to pass Razil to get to Lyss, but Razil stopped him short with her saber.

"Not so fast," she said as she swung the blade at him.

He yelled in frustration and began attacking her fiercely, his blade flashing in the firelight as he moved this way and that. Razil blocked his attacks with difficulty, gritting her teeth as the impact reverberated up her arms. Wolf's speed matched his strength, making him a difficult opponent.

Out of the corner of her eyes, Razil saw Lyss sneak down the rockface towards the men fighting the dragon. She hoped she would make it. Or else all was for naught.

Razil took the offensive and lunged towards Wolf's side. He spun at the last moment and let the blade pass before striking at her in return. Razil threw herself backward and felt a whisper of the blade tickle her neck. Muscles straining, she straightened and struck again, only to be blocked with Wolf's short sword, her hand shuddering under the force of the blow.

Razil risked a glance at Lyss and saw her make it down the rockface and move towards Crimshyrbane, who was unleashing flames that Blayne and Drack barely dodged. Her momentary lapse in focus cost her. Wolf's sword sliced through her bicep. She yelped, agony burning like fire up her arm. The magic of her amulet began to repair the wound, but the pain was there nonetheless.

She refocused, narrowing her eyes and taking a defensive stance with her saber. She would not let Wolf get the better of her. Finally, she would have her revenge on the man who took advantage of her when she was young, turning her to crime because she had no other options.

"You done playing the hero, Razil? You know you will never beat me in a sword fight. It's not too late to join my cause," Wolf taunted with a raised brow.

"I may not be a hero, but I will certainly never join you," Razil spat back.

"Then I shall enjoy watching your last breath," Wolf said as he lunged forward again with a thrashing strike. Razil barely parried in time, and the force of it made her stumble back.

Wolf pushed her further and further back, cutting and thrusting his sword forward. Sweat clung to Razil's brow, her arms shaking with the force of each parry.

Wolf slashed at her again, and she dropped her saber, crying out as her wrist flared with pain. Heart hammering, she held her arms open and, with a pleading look, begged, "Please. Don't do this."

Wolf smirked as he prowled closer, enjoying the agonizing pursuit of his prey. He stalked forward and drove his sword towards Razil's abdomen. At the same time, she bit down on her back molar and spat blinding powder in his eyes. He dropped his sword in shock, groping at his eyes as he howled in surprise.

Razil lunged forward and tackled him to the ground. They fell with a shattering thud, and Wolf gasped out a pained breath. He reached up toward Razil's neck, but she maneuvered out of the way and grabbed her knife, which she always kept hidden on her calf. She unsheathed the sharp blade and slid it across Wolf's neck.

Gurgling a pained cry, he squirmed and sputtered, wriggling at her feet. She stood watching him, reveling in the sight. Finally, the predator of Gar was no more. Satisfaction coursed through her every vein as she watched him struggle to his end.

Distant yelling interrupted her victory, and she turned to look at the mayhem below. The red dragon was growing tired of the games. His flames grew stronger, and it was evident that her friends would not last much longer.

Razil sprinted to the edge and descended the sharp rock face. Her bicep still ached from where Wolf had cut it earlier, but she paid it no attention. She climbed down with every ounce of her strength. When she reached the ground, Razil saw Lyss trying to sneak up on the dragon from behind.

Crimshyrbane was occupied trying to burn Zippy, who was playing a sound that seemed to provide a halo of protection around himself. The flames licked around the orb stemming from his lute as Blayne and Drack attempted to get close enough to strike the dragon with their weapons. Razil darted forward to try to join the fight.

Lyss was almost within striking distance with Dragon's Bane. The necklace and blade shone a brighter red the closer she got to Crimshyrbane. Razil joined Blayne and Drack, and the three of them advanced slowly in front of the dragon, trying to keep his attention on them.

Just as Lyss was about to strike, Crimshyrbane turned his massive head and narrowed his eyes at the blade in Lyss' hand. He inhaled deeply, ready to release a flame at Lyss. Razil panicked and threw her bloodied dagger at the dragon's torso.

He turned out of anger and released his flame at Razil instead. She was engulfed by it. The heat burned her skin even as the amulet around her neck tried to mitigate the damage. Dragon's fire may have been too much for the amulet to handle. Razil would take death gladly if it meant Lyss was safe, though. She stood in the flame, basking in its pain, until all of a sudden it stopped.

The flame vanished from around her body, and a loud thump shook in Razil's ears. Crimshyrbane lay flat with his serpent eyes lolling back lifelessly. Lyss stood covered in blood as she removed the Dragon's Bane from his heart.

Before Razil could fully comprehend what had happened, Lyss rushed to her side and grabbed her chin. Razil's skin felt tight as her amulet struggled to heal her scorched skin. She winced as Lyss ran her hand over her face, but tried to ignore the pain.

"Do not ever do something like that again," Lyss demanded as she stared into her eyes.

"Save you?" Razil questioned as she let herself sink into Lyss' dark eyes.

"Sacrifice yourself!" Lyss screamed.

"I can't make any promises," Razil smirked as her legs wobbled beneath her. Her body felt weak even as her amulet tried to heal her.

Lyss moved in closer, holding her up in her arms, and crashed her lips into Razil's. She pulled back and whispered, "I love you, you absolute fool."

Before Razil could speak, Blayne, Drack, and Zippy ran over and wrapped them both in a group hug. It was sweaty, bloody, and she was sure it smelled atrocious. But she was so happy she didn't care. They had done it. The dragon had been slain, and they could return to claim their prize. Razil was elated and, for once, at peace.

CHAPTER 25

PARCHMENT AND SEAL

Razil could hardly believe her eyes when she saw the large stone gates of Gar Thanik. The journey had been long. It had felt like forever, when in reality, it was probably mere weeks.

The large stone walls were lined with archers standing tall, looking like statues. The midday sun shone down on the ballista positioned at the top of the wall near the entrance gate. Archers pulled their strings taut until Razil pulled back a corner of the cloth bundle held in Dracklin's arms, revealing the red dragon's head. The bundle weighed so much that he was the only one strong enough to hold it alone. Everyone else had to take turns in pairs.

The metal gate creaked and opened with haste as knights rushed from behind. When they got closer, it was evident that they hadn't slept since Crimshyrbane's threat, all of them boasting unshaven beards and dark, circled eyes. But life seemed to fill the soldiers at the sight of the severed dragon's head.

They were ushered straight to the castle. The whole city seemed to be holding its breath, waiting for the dragon to return and claim their lives. People moved slowly and somberly, preparing the city for siege. As they saw the dragon's head, liveliness entered their movements as they pointed and abandoned their tasks. Crowds formed around them, their whispers buzzing like a beehive.

The stone on the castle looked like it had been haphazardly shoved back in place, and they had not bothered to rebuild the councilor's quarters yet. Razil assumed they thought it pointless to rebuild if the dragon was to return. So, the whole city waited on bated breath for an unlikely savior or a likely destroyer.

Lyss grabbed Razil's hand and squeezed as they awaited the king. The warmth of her palm spread all the way to her chest. Moments felt like hours as they stood there. The entire city seemed to share the same sentiment. Could it be? Could these unlikely travelers be the answer to their prayers?

The large castle door creaked open as knights ushered someone out into the daylight. But it was not the king. Genna Landcaster stood with teary eyes and a tattered dress, staring at them from the castle's entrance. Her eyes were shadowed with dark rings, and she looked impossibly tired.

"Alyssandra?" Genna asked as she looked at them.

"Mom," Lyss whispered.

Councilor Landcaster sprinted towards them, wrapping her daughter in a hug. Only then did Lyss release Razil's hand. Finally, Genna Landcaster pulled back and asked, "Could it be?"

Lyss nodded as she guided her mother over to Drack. The councilor gasped in horror at the sight of the lifeless head, then a look of relief washed over her face.

"Crimshyrbane is no more," Lyss said.

"Is it true? The dragon is dead?" a weary voice asked.

Razil looked up to see the king. His hair seemed grayer and his beard longer than the last time she had seen him.

Razil bowed her head and said, "King Luvian, we present the red dragon's head to you." Drack raised the head higher for all to see as she spoke.

The king shouted in glee at the sight, and all of Gar Thanik joined him, releasing a collective breath of relief. The following moments moved so rapidly she could hardly keep up. Beer was thrust into her hand by Wes. Her aunt and uncle appeared from the crowd, hugging her and Blayne tightly.

Music erupted, and dancing broke out right there in front of the castle.

In the middle of the dancing a squire procured a piece of parchment that was a deed to a portion of Gar. The king stood expectantly, waiting for Razil to sign.

"Gar Razil comes to fruition at last," Zippy said as he handed her a quill.

Razil looked to Lyss and shook her head. She realized she did not want Gar Razil. She did not want a position where she had complete power as a ruler. If that were the case, it would end up the same as Gar Thanik. Because the truth of the matter was, when all the power was in one hand, even the best of hands, it would eventually sour.

"No," Razil said as she shook her head.

Her friends looked at her in confusion, so she continued, "No, this will be Gar Solace—a place for all who want peace and prosperity for all. I do not want to rule. I want to serve and be a part of a better kind of community."

Lyss came up next to her and kissed her on the cheek. "I like that," she said warmly, her eyes sparkling with love. Razil felt something bloom in her chest.

"So, you will join me?" Razil asked hesitantly.

"Of course. You will need someone to help you manage politics with the other provinces of Gar," Lyss said with a wink.

This was a chance for a new beginning. A chance for a new love with Lyss, away from Gar Thanik, where they could heal. An opportunity to build something kind. An opportunity to build a place for people to come and have a second chance. Gar Solace would be a fresh start for them all.

CHAPTER 26

EVER AFTER

FIVE YEARS LATER...

The years following the death of the red dragon had gone by in a blur. It was magical and amazing, yet balanced with careful planning and frequent growing pains. But Gar Solace had proven to be worth the work.

It was a haven for all who wanted to live in a way that benefited everyone. It was a community built on the tenets of love, and communal health and wellness came before wealth and personal gain.

People had moved from all over Gar to live in such a place, some even from Sharkstown and Leedbriar. It was a diverse town full of vibrant culture and all kinds of people, and that is what made it so great, in Zippy's opinion. Everyone contributed their talents and gifts. Though not everyone got along, everyone respected that this was a place where all were welcome and had value.

The first several years required a lot of building: homes from wood and thatch, a communal garden in the center of town, and a well that provided fresh water. It was all hands on deck to build a place like this, and even Zippy rolled up his sleeves and got his hands dirty.

He helped build the tavern and a room for himself near the bar. It was a small space, but it had plenty of room for a fluffy bed, all his books, and his kind of cat, Pumpkin, whom he brought from Gar Thanik. He played almost every night at the tavern, but instead of collecting coin, he now played for the joy of it. He sometimes added magic to give people a warm fuzziness in their chest, but sometimes he played without magic just to enjoy the music.

His friends had thrived as well. Alyssandra and several others who joined from around Gar led Gar Solace. Alyssandra was a fair and just leader, and all decisions were made as a unit rather than by the individual. They still answered to the king, but he allowed them plenty of space to make things their own, as he did the other territories of Gar.

Razil and Alyssandra lived in a small wooden cottage with wooden walls that was always bursting with life and color from the many plants Alyssandra kept collecting. Razil worked as a blacksmith in a small smithy behind their cottage. Alyssandra urged her to join the leadership council, but Razil realized all she ever wanted was to live a simple life among friends.

And so, she did. Dessbelle and Razil's aunt and uncle moved to Gar Solace and helped her with the smithy. Her mother remained in Gar Thanik, and though it concerned Razil, she could not change her. They often hosted family dinners, and Zippy joined along with Dracklin and Blayne. Alyssandra and Razil were the kind of couple that had their ups and downs but worked through them in a safe and healing way.

The two married last year, and the ceremony was quaint and beautiful. To see them grow through pain and distrust to tenderness and forgiving love was unlike anything Zippy had ever seen. Dracklin was the only one at the wedding who cried more than Zippy.

Speaking of Dracklin, he and Blayne finally stopped tiptoeing around each other and started courting. They lived in a small one-bedroom cottage outside their town's barracks where their local militia trains. Blayne was the general there, and Dracklin trained the militia in hand-to-hand combat. They had to deal with the occasional goblin raids; otherwise, it was relatively quiet.

Everything was well, but one thing wasn't. Through the years, Zippy realized he had run too many times to count. He ran because he feared disappointment and didn't know how to let people down. So, he'd always escaped before he had the chance.

He packed his bags on a quest to face that fear and make amends for how he left. But this time, when he left Gar Solace for the journey, he told his friends where he was going with the promise of returning and even had a going-away party.

But as he stood here today, his heart thumped painfully in his chest. His parents' burrow looked the same as when he'd left it: a small wooden door tucked into a gentle grass hill, with a sign that read "Redbeard" and a small rabbit emblem next to it.

He knocked softly twice, and the warm wood tingled against his knuckles. Before he could knock again, the door was pulled open, and a face appeared that looked familiar to his own. The man's cheeks were rounded like his, and his beard was a fiery red, just greyer. His eyes were a bright green with slightly more wrinkles framing the outside.

"My son," the man blurted in a watery tone, and before Zippy could respond, he was pulled into an embrace so tight he feared he wouldn't be able to breathe much longer.

"Dad, I can't breathe," Zippy managed to gasp.

"Sorry, I just can't believe my eyes," he said as he released Zippy.

Before Zippy could respond, Zippy's father had his arm around his shoulders and was pulling him through their home. He was dragged through the sitting room, which smelled of his father's tobacco and berry pies, where a game of marbles sat at the wooden table in the center. It looked exactly like it did when he'd left it, but Zippy did not have time to ponder the nostalgia as he was pulled into the kitchen.

There he found his mother with her back to him, bent over a wood-burning stove, making what smelled like a delicious pie. The clay wall in front of her boasted a great number of sprouting carrots, and wooden cabinets were filled to the brim with flour and mixing pots. Candles burned and flickered from their resting places in between her baking mess.

"Shendar, look who I have," Zippy's father said.

"Clide, tell your friends they'll have to wait. Pie needs a bit longer," she replied.

"Mom," Zippy squeaked out.

His mother stopped and straightened before turning around. Her round eyes were full of tears that streamed down flour-caked cheeks. She rushed over to him and put her hands on his face.

"Could it be?" she asked.

"It's me. Mom and Dad, I am sorry it's been so long," Zippy said.

"Nonsense, do not apologize. Oh, how I've waited for this day," his mother said as she hugged him.

Zippy's nerves melted in her arms. Eventually, they all moved to the sitting room and sat in small wooden chairs with carefully crocheted blankets draped over them. Zippy wrapped one around his shoulders like he'd done as a child. And he talked. He talked and he talked and he talked about everything and nothing. He told them where he'd been and the adventures he'd had.

And his parents listened. They listened and did not chasten him once for leaving.

"Why did you never visit us or write?" Zippy's father eventually asked when Zippy had finished, hurt evident in his eyes.

"Because I felt like a disappointment," Zippy said.

"Then, son, I am the disappointment. I am so sorry for putting pressure on you to be a certain way. We love who you are and want you to be yourself," his father said.

"You are perfect just the way you are and have turned out to be a wonderful gnome," his mother added.

"Thank you," Zippy said, and now it was his time for tears.

His mother left the room and returned with a pie in her hand. They ate and chatted some more. This time, they told Zippy about the happenings of Berry Meadows, and though it sounded as if not much had changed, it was nice to hear.

"I cannot stay here long," Zippy said, and it was bitter sweat.

"I know," Zippy's mother said.

"But I will return and write this time," Zippy said, and he meant it.

"We love you so much, son. Nothing would make us happier," his father replied.

So, they ate pies and talked, and Zippy was taken back to a time of his youth. But this time, instead of feeling shame, he felt like himself. It wasn't going to be perfect, but it was a start. Zippy could not wait for what the future held and what adventure he would go on next.

Acknowledgements

First and foremost I want to say thank you to Fiona. Your editing expertise really took my story to the next level! I could not have done it without you. For the stunning cover I would like to thank Zal art. You really brought my vision to life! Also, I would like to say thank you to my wife, Veronica. Thank you for believing in my dreams and encouraging me.

About the Author

Sheridan Gillam was born and raised in Texas and loves all things BBQ and crawfish. She also loves fantasy and science fiction and can often be found daydreaming in her own world. She lives for a sunny day out on the water in her kayak. She resides in a small coastal town with her wife, son, and rescue animals. Follow her @SNG_reads on both Instagram and TikTok.

Other works by this author:

- Scrooge You, Emily Tompkins!

Coming Soon:

- The Water Dragon's Paladin

www.ingramcontent.com/pod-product-compliance
Lightning Source LLC
Chambersburg PA
CBHW050332110726
47899CB00007B/2470